Praise for *Shep and the King of Hearts*

This emotional story of love, loss, and redemption explores the silent harm that gambling addictions can do to a family.
—*Dan Trolaro,* VP of Prevention,
EPIC Global Solutions

Shep and the King of Hearts is a touching novel that explores the pain of addiction with a gentle hand. Stacy weaves a tale of forgiveness, redemption, restoration, and hope through the story of one broken man, his estranged daughter, and a chaplain named Shep who pursues them both with a love inspired by God. A lovely romance, a lovely story, a lovely read!
—*Heidi Chiavaroli,* Two-Time Carol Award–Winning
Author of *The Orchard House* and *The Way Back*

In *Shep and the King of Hearts,* Stacy Ladyman crafts a compelling tale focused on faith and forgiveness for a family dealing with the wounds of gambling addiction. This compelling novella will grab readers and keep them invested in the story to discover how Shep, an unusual and charming chaplain, will help Chris and Jim resolve issues that have burdened this father and daughter for years.
—*Carrie Turansky,* Award-Winning Author of
The Legacy of Longdale Manor and *A Token of Love*

Relatively few novels cover gambling addiction, in comparison to other forms of addiction, already making *Shep and the King of Hearts* notable. Readers who embrace Ladyman's creation and her characters' journeys will find a vivid depiction of Jim's gambling life and the loving family that turns to God for help in bringing him back home. Ultimately, it's not just a story of struggling with destructive urges and behavior patterns but a tale of love.

—*Midwest Book Review*

SHEP

AND THE

KING OF HEARTS

SHEP
AND THE
KING OF
HEARTS

STACY J. LADYMAN

Published by Redemption Press, PO Box 427, Enumclaw, WA 98022, (360) 226-3488.

Redemption Press is honored to present this title in partnership with the author. The views expressed or implied in this work are those of the author. Redemption Press provides our imprint seal representing design excellence, creative content, and high-quality production.

This is a work of fiction. Names, characters, businesses, places, events, and incidents in this book are either the products of the author's imagination or used in a fictitious manner. Any resemblance to actual persons, living or dead, or actual events is purely coincidental.

Scriptures taken from the Holy Bible, New International Version®, NIV®. Copyright © 1973, 1978, 1984, 2011 by Biblica, Inc.™ Used by permission of Zondervan. All rights reserved worldwide. www.zondervan.com. The "NIV" and "New International Version" are trademarks registered in the United States Patent and Trademark Office by Biblica, Inc.™

ISBN 13: 979-8-218-45355-8 (Paperback)
979-8-218-45357-2 (eBook)

Library of Congress Catalog Card Number: 2024909979

To Papa

My grandfather, Tom Whiteside, was a banker. He began as a bookkeeper and retired as chairman of the board of our hometown bank. He then became a poet and published four books. How blessed our whole family was for it! This book is dedicated to you, Papa. You and Mama Grayce gave us a lifeline with which we could rebuild our lives in the warmth of your love. I am eternally grateful and proud to be your granddaughter.

Compose a Song
and Leave All Grief Behind

Compose a song and leave all grief behind
And send it forth to find a grieving heart
So you can be of comfort to mankind.

Discover treasures built into your mind,
Your own uniqueness given to impart:
Compose a song and leave all grief behind.

Break free of melancholy moods that bind
And pluck resentments out, each poisoned dart,
So you can be of comfort to mankind.

Take time each day to contemplate and find
The sounds of music where true rhythms start:
Compose a song and leave all grief behind.

Allow Love's mysteries, though all unsigned,
To speak their music through you as an art.
So you can be of comfort to mankind.

And thank your Muse, your listening ear inclined.
For granting words as from a master chart:
Compose a song and leave all grief behind
So you can be of comfort to mankind.

Tom Whiteside
The House of Love

CONTENTS

PREFACE

In 2016, on a snowy December night, I drove to hear a talk given at a church thirty minutes from my home. A few weeks prior, an advertising flyer for a presentation entitled "Gambling: The Hidden Addiction," sponsored by the Council on Compulsive Gambling of New Jersey, caught my attention. A picture of poker cards and chips bordered the flyer.

I arrived at the stone church with red doors and walked to the entrance under powdery white flakes. Upon entering, I did not immediately see anyone, but I heard Christmas hymns softly playing. I followed the music to the beautiful sanctuary. Heavy wooden trusses formed the vaulted ceiling. Christmas decorations adorned the altar. I listened to the recorded music for a moment. The soothing melodies calmed my fears. Fears of coming here in the first place. Fears of listening to a talk about the very thing that had changed my life and severed a crucial relationship for me some forty years earlier. Why was I here? Why had I come? As strong as the urge to come here for this talk was, there was now an even stronger urge to get up and walk out.

Instead, I crossed the hallway and entered the meeting room with signs posted for the presentation. I was the only woman in the room; approximately four men stood at the front. They looked a little surprised that I, this middle-aged woman, would be out on such a winter's night to listen to a talk about gambling addiction. They were gracious and came over to greet me. I met the pastor and a few others and then was introduced to Dan Trolaro, our speaker for the evening. I would soon learn he was a father and himself a man in recovery from a gambling addiction.

I took my seat and listened to Dan's story. It was heart-wrenching. Afterward, the group got up and spoke to one another. At first, others might have thought I was in recovery myself, but I explained to them that I was thinking of writing a book that dealt with this issue, and that was why I had come. I nervously told them that it was my father who had a gambling addiction. They formed a circle around me and prayed for my book and story, and I was so thankful. Thankful that I had come out on this December night. I will never forget those prayers.

I would like to tell you I came home and began tapping this novel out on my computer the next day. But the opposite is true. Instead, fear had me gripped. Somehow, Dan's story was like my father's story. Very different circumstances, but this ugly thing called a gambling addiction had affected my family, just as it had Dan's. I was saddened. Dan and I agreed to have coffee, which we did a few times, but still, it would take me many years to come to grips with my grief—the grief of what I had lost as a child, the loss of a father. There was also the fear of examining my own heart to write this story. After all, some of my feelings had been locked up for a very long time. Maybe that's why fiction is the perfect balm. It helps us cope, using fictional circumstances so that we can examine, learn, and grow in our real-life experiences.

Thank you, Dan Trolaro, for sharing your story on that snowy night years ago. Dan now works for EPIC Global Solutions as the VP of Prevention, traveling across the country, telling his story, and educating students and athletes about the potential for gambling-related harms. You, Dan, are a reminder that we all have a voice—a voice to help others, even when it is hard.

I hope this fictional story will speak to you about truths of the heart, because every human heart, addicted or not, needs to be loved.

God bless you, and thank you for reading,

—Stacy

CHAPTER 1

3W

The sun was low as Jim stopped the truck and got out to open the steel ranch gate, his black cowboy boots crunching the dirt. It was a crisp summer night in the hill country of Idaho. Tumbleweeds whipped across the sagebrush mountain as the arid sky turned into an orange sunset.

Chris and her dad drove through the gate and rattled their way up the hill of the ranch. Towering Rocky Mountain peaks stood in the background. The radio on the '57 Ford truck played "I Just Can't Help Believing" by B. J. Thomas.

"What will we do at our ranch tonight, Dad?"

"Well, it's not exactly our ranch. Mr. Struthers owns it. We've got to check on a momma horse that's probably ready to have her foal. I guess you've never seen a horse have a baby, Chris?"

Chris shook her little auburn head no. The ruffle trim of her pink-flowered short set was soft on her legs compared to her skinned-up knees. She had taken a few falls from her Schwinn bike lately. Chris could barely see from the front windshield at eight, but pushing herself up occasionally to spot the Indian paintbrush flowers was a must. She loved the red ones.

"Well, I think tonight is the night."

Chris could feel those bubbles in her stomach again, like when she heard her mom, Helen, arguing with her dad about why he was always out playing cards. Those times were scary bubbles because she didn't like how their voices sounded, but these bubbles were excited ones for the new baby horse. Chris knew the difference.

As they continued up the road, she looked at her dad and asked, "What color is she?"

"The mare? Oh. She's a black mare, a spade, just like the poker card. Chris, hand me my Skoal. It's in the slot by the cigarette lighter."

Chris reached for the familiar can and handed it to him. Jim twisted the tab, released the seal, took a tobacco dip out of the round green container, and lodged the minty goop next to his gum. He screwed the top back on and tossed it on the seat next to a deck of cards, and a few blue and red poker chips fell to the floor. Chris reached down and picked them up, rubbing the ridges of one of the blue chips between her fingers.

Jim looked at the poker chip and then out to the road. "You know, Chris, I brand each cow and horse we have on this ranch. I mark them with a *W* for Warren. This way, I always know my cattle. We are all *W*s, our family. Your momma is thinking about leaving me and breaking up our little family. We can't let that happen. I'm gonna brand this new colt with a 3W. That's what it's always going to be. Right, Chris? The three Warrens. Nothing is ever going to change that."

They parked at Struthers's cabin. Not far from it stood the small barn and stall. Jim came around to help Chris out of the truck. He opened the door, put his arm out for her, and pulled her tight.

"Come on, Spud"—his Idaho nickname for Chris. "Let's see how the momma is doing."

She looked into his hazel eyes and put her hand flat on his crew cut to feel its brush. Her face rubbed against his whiskers, and the smell of tobacco filled her nostrils. Jim whirled Chris out of the seat and onto the ground. Her pink cowboy boots landed safely on the rocky soil.

The mare was walking round and round nervously in her stall. Jim walked over and pulled a string light on as dusk approached. He went into the hay-covered booth and began to steady her, coaxing her to lie down. Chris climbed halfway up the stall gate, steadied her feet on one of the slats, and flung the rest of her tiny body over the side to watch.

"Steady, girl. We're here now. You look ready to do this. Just as I thought. Come on now, lay down, girl."

The mare's stomach convulsed with each contraction. Jim stood by her, knelt, and stroked her belly. Half vet, half rancher.

"This foal is breach." Jim spit his tobacco on the hay, along with a few choice words.

"What's that? What does that mean?" Chris swallowed hard.

"It's when the baby is coming out the wrong way. I got to turn her, Chris. If I don't, we'll lose her and the foal. Grab that horse blanket from the next stall and lay it on the ground. Quick!"

Her heart pounded as she flung open the latch and ran for the ribbed blue blanket. She stretched it out on the floor as best as she could next to the horse's backside and hurried out of the birthing stall. Quivering in a fetal position, low on the dirt, she shut her eyes tight for a minute. The smell of hay was strong, and her dad's bad words were coming out fast. She forced her eyes open and peered through the bottom opening of the gate. It was night now. She looked at the yellow glow of light over the stall and felt a little warmer.

She watched as her father's hands went into the horse carefully but with gut strength, the mare wheezing in pain. Chris put her head down between her knees and muffled her ears from hearing any more. There was a lot of blood and what seemed like goo. Steam rose from the hay floor. She gasped at seeing a little black-and-white baby horse suddenly out and on the hay before her. The little filly was wobbling on stick legs that looked like pogo sticks. Her markings of black and white were so perfect that Chris was sure she could never color a horse picture as beautiful as that.

Rubbing his hands clean on a cloth, Jim smiled with satisfaction. "There she is, Spud. There is our 3W."

CHAPTER 2

1995—Twenty-Five Years Later

"Shep to maintenance." The hospital intercom blasted over the grounds near the Hopewell Hill entrance sign that read, *A Place for Healing.* The announcement came again. "Shep to maintenance."

"Wonder what Hector and the boys need their chaplain for today?" Shep walked from the cafeteria's back entrance with his hot coffee in hand and sat down in his golf cart to take a sip. Riker, his black-and-white Border collie, was waiting in the back seat for his morning biscuit. With one gulp, Riker devoured the cheese-covered sausage delight.

Shep put the golf cart in gear and got his waving hand ready. A bumper sticker that read *Wave to the Preacher,* which the boys in the maintenance shed had affixed as a ruse, kept him busy waving hello to patients and staff. Peacocks fanned their blue, green, and brown feathers in the middle of the pathway as Shep gave a gentle honk to prod them along. A fountain spewed water into the little pond on the behavioral hospital's sixty-acre property.

He pulled up to the weathered red barn turned-maintenance department, grabbed his coffee, and headed inside. Riker followed Shep to the center of the barn, where two men in coveralls were working with wrenches and screwdrivers on an oversized air conditioner. Greasy tools were scattered around, and the smell of diesel and cigarettes filled the air.

"Can I ask why you boys needed me so much as to call me over early this morning?"

Hector quickly mused from the compressor, "Morning, Shep. We called you here because Bob needs prayer. His golf game is off."

They burst into laughter.

"Oh, this sounds critical." Shep walked over to the side of the shed, where a bag of dusty golf clubs hung on a hook. With a look of mischief, he pulled out a driver. He tapped the club on the palm of his hand. "Well, maybe you need to watch and learn. Follow me," he said.

Hector and the boys left their work and followed him as he walked out of the mechanic's barn and across the gravel driveway to the edge of a grassy field. Shep set the ball on a tee and lined up his tall, muscular body perfectly perpendicular to the tee.

With full force, *swoosh*, he struck the ball. The hollow sound of his club hitting the ball had the tune of pure power.

The ploy to get attention from their much-loved chaplain had worked. They sipped some coffee and talked about the latest basketball game. They visited for a while before the next call for Shep came over the intercom.

"Shep to Admin. Shep to Admin."

"Administration!" Bob blurted out. "What did you do now, Shep? You're in trouble again! If the boss lady is calling you, she's gonna have a piece of you now."

Shep's olive skin turned red. "Must be some paperwork I haven't filled out. No worries." He bid the boys goodbye, left Riker with them, and drove off across campus. The American flag waved in the breeze, and freshly planted pansies edged the front of the administration building. As he entered, his feet squished the beige padded carpeting in the business office hallway.

Gently tapping on the door under the name plate Chris Warren, Shep peered in. Chris was on the phone, but she waved for him to come in. Shep crept in and sat in a leather chair while she finished her call.

"Spencer, I have to cancel our dinner plans for tonight. I've had something pressing come up. Yes, I'll fill you in later." She hung up the phone, folded her slender, manicured hands on the desk, and leaned over it. "How are you doing, Shep?"

"I'm fine, just fine." Shep ran his hand over his thick chestnut hair.

"Shep, I'll be straight to the point," Chris said with a familiar edge to her voice. She cleared her throat and fixed the collar on her starched white blouse. "You have got to stop goofing off with the maintenance guys. The chaplain playing golf in the middle of the morning doesn't look so good. Really."

"How did you know my whereabouts this morning?"

"Shep, people see you out and around all the time. I have eyes all over this hospital."

"Well, I was only spending some time with the boys."

"Another thing: Have you produced the ecumenical report? I do need to keep a census on our religious diversity, Shep."

"I am getting to that ... today."

"The board asks for it to be added to the quarterly report. Can you fill out the forms as we previously discussed after each visit you make? It will make your life easier; then you can transfer that information to the report I requested, all in a simple Excel spreadsheet."

"All in an easy Excel sheet," Shep said as his eyes widened.

She rose from her chair and faced the window with her back to Shep. Her worsted wool blue suit accented her slim figure.

Sighing, she said, "Shep, on to another matter. I have a problem."

"Okay." *The all-star girl has a problem?*

She glanced back at Shep, making eye contact with him, and then turned back toward the window as if embarrassed to face him when the words came out. "I have a father I haven't seen in twenty-five years."

"Why, Chris, I had no idea."

She paced past the wooden credenza displaying New Jersey Hospital awards for the top administrator. She held her hand up behind her like a crossing guard monitor saying stop. Still facing the window, she kept her back to Shep. "Please, let me get this out. My father is a gambler. We hear he has lived like a nomad since Mom and I left. He called me out of the blue last night and is coming to New Jersey." Chris turned to face Shep, tears pooling in her green eyes like high tide. "His name is Jim, Jim Warren. He's coming on a Greyhound bus that gets here Friday. I have arranged for him to stay at the Crown Hotel in Hopewell."

"Chris, maybe this is a chance to reconnect with your father."

"Maybe. I hope that's true. But when I told Jim on the phone that he missed everything—my growing up, my high school graduation, my going to college—all he could say was, 'That's the way the cookie crumbles.'"

She blinked and cocked her head as she straightened her suit. "Here's what we are going to do," she said in her administrator's voice, resuming control of herself and the situation. "I will put him up if he agrees to come here for some counseling sessions I will cover."

"How can I help? If there's anything you need, just say it. I'll never forget what you did for me, bringing me here through the chaplaincy program from prison. Then when Annie got sick ..." Shep shook his head, looking downward. "Hot meals and flowers showing up at our house every week." Shep moved in a little closer, sitting on the edge of his chair. With his words, he tapped his finger on the edge of her desk in unison. "Let me know if you need anything with your Jim, and I'll do it. I mean, anything."

Chris smiled. "Befriend him, watch out for him, take him for rides in your golf cart. I don't know, just whatever you can do between counseling sessions."

"No golf games on the lawn?"

"No! And let's keep this between us."

He had heard that anticipatory tone in her voice before, more before a presentation to the board, but this time it was personal.

"Aye, aye, sir ... ma'am." He saluted, turned on his heel, and left the room.

CHAPTER 3

Santa Claus Cowboy

The Greyhound bus originated in Las Vegas. Making several connections, it was on the last leg of the journey, arriving late from Pittsburg to New Jersey. Chris sat alone on a stone bench outside the station, waiting for it, waiting for Jim.

"Station arrivals ..." The shrill station bell and announcement signaling a bus was arriving caused Chris to look up at the arrival and departure board. The Las Vegas bus was still en route. She ran her fingers through her auburn hair and uncrossed her legs carefully in her navy pencil skirt. Nervously, she put the toe of her pump on a twig and rolled it on the ground.

Chris fell back into her thoughts and the phone call she had received from Jim just days ago.

"Hey, Spud. Your dad here. I ... I'm coming to town."

Spud was a name she hadn't heard in so long. Jim had given her that nickname when they went to the potato farms after the harvest, and the local farmers let families pick up the remainder of the crop.

"Jim, you're coming to town?"

"Yeah, I have some unfinished business."

Jim gave Chris the bus arrival information just before the pay phone cut them off, leaving Chris with only a dial tone.

As she stared at a piece of green chewing gum flattened on the pavement in front of her, thoughts of the days before she and her mother left Jim and the redbrick house on Alta Drive came flooding into her mind. She was almost nine.

Chris had some good memories in that house from twenty-five years ago. She remembered listening to her first album, the Beatles' *Let It Be*, in her bedroom with red flocked wallpaper and fleur-de-lis designs. Many times, as she listened to the music and danced around the room, the sheer white curtains moved like a dance partner in the breeze from an open window. Other times, Chris overheard her parents arguing in their bedroom next door as she combed her doll's brown hair.

"Jim, we are leaving for good," Helen said.

"Go on and run back to your daddy," Jim snarled.

"I am not running back to my father. I'm leaving you for the good of Chris."

"For a few debts I owe? I'll make that back in no time, plus some."

"You can't argue, Jim. You've got to admit you're in trouble, your gambling debts are only mounting, and our bank account is nearly empty."

"I'll make a million dollars, and then you'll see; you'll wish you stayed with me then."

"Money is not the object, Jim. It's our life. We are losing everything," Mom tried to whisper in their bedroom.

Eventually, the morning of their departure arrived. There was no more arguing. The air seemed heavy, and a pall had taken over the house. As Chris lay in bed before sunrise, she heard the drip from the hall bathroom faucet, every droplet hitting the rusty ring in the porcelain sink, a bell tolling the end of their life in Idaho with Jim.

Helen came into Chris's room early so they could get a start on driving across the country. They moved around the house like mice, afraid to trip a mousetrap that would snap and wake Jim. They loaded all they had in the green Vega station wagon. Her father never got up to say goodbye. They packed up, drove away, and slipped out of Jim's life.

Looking up from the pavement, Chris checked her black Movado watch as dusk approached, thinking how late Jim was. She looked up at the arrival board again. This time the words Las Vegas were flashing. She turned to the right toward the parking lot entrance, and an oncoming bus's headlights shone toward her.

The wheels on the Greyhound turned in front of Chris's bench, and the air brakes decompressed as the bus came to a stop. The door opened with a screech, and the first passengers began to descend.

His dusty black cowboy boots touched the ground. Chris took in every part of him. She recognized her father, except this man had a white beard, and his skin was windburned. He wore dirty jeans tattered at the seams and a worn leather belt. The tarnished belt buckle was engraved with the initial J. His faded blue shirt with two pockets had glasses hanging out of one and a bulging billfold in the other. Then, his face. His hazel eyes sparkled with mischief. He looked like a Santa Claus cowboy.

She got up slowly from her bench and walked toward him. "Jim?"

"Chris." Jim smiled, and as he looked at her, she thought his eyes relaxed for a moment. "Well, you've grown up!"

"Yes, that's what twenty-five years will do," she said as she shook his hand awkwardly and examined his now-wrinkled face.

"Guess so."

"My car is over here. Where are your bags?"

"Oh, don't have much. I like to travel light," he said in his burly voice that all could hear. He carried a duffel bag in his hand.

They walked to Chris's car.

"Well, this is nice," he said, eyeing her Lexus. "Bet you had to pay a pretty piece for this hunk."

He opened the door and gave the interior a good look.

"It gets me where I'm going," Chris said.

Jim sighed when he got into the front seat. "I tell you, that bus driver didn't know where he was going. The trip from Nevada is long enough, but when we left Pittsburgh, that little runt of a driver couldn't find his way out of a paper bag."

Chris swallowed hard. "Well, you're here now. I'm going to take you to the Crown Hotel downtown. You might remember it."

"Yeah, I remember it, but I thought you might be able to put me up. Not sure what that place is charging. Always was a dump."

"Well, they've remodeled it; it's nice and clean now. Don't worry, Jim. I've prepaid the week for you until we sort things out."

"Oh, now you don't have to do that. I can pay my way." A sense of relief took over his face. He took his billfold from his pocket and pulled out the bus itinerary. "This schedule isn't worth the paper it's printed on." He slipped his empty billfold back into his pocket.

They drove past the city park. "Well, it doesn't look like Hopewell has changed much."

"Not too much," Chris said.

They parked and entered the hotel lobby. The new hardwood floors gleamed. The battered old red-and-white Crown Hotel sign, with a red crown graphic, hung as a piece of nostalgia behind the restored front desk. A fire crackled in the white-painted brick fireplace, surrounded by comfortable plaid sofas. A set of tables and chairs were to the left. "This place doesn't even look the same," Jim said.

"Yes, sir, we restored it, top to bottom," the teenage front desk clerk responded. "You're in room 210 up those stairs there." He motioned toward a maple staircase with a polished black railing.

Chris and Jim went up and turned the corner to his room. Chris turned the lock with the antique key, and they stepped inside.

"Nice and clean, modern conveniences. It ain't like my camper."

Chris sat down in a wing chair. "Jim, I want you to understand a few things. You can stay here on one condition. I was hoping you could have some meetings with a few of my colleagues. I work at a hospital."

"I used to work at a hospital, one of my side jobs, for a while. Those nurses were real hussies. They wanted me to be a maintenance man, well below my pay grade, so I worked for a few weeks and left. Don't know how you work with those nurse types."

"I'm in charge of a lot of nurses. I run a hospital."

"You do? Well, how do you like that? A daughter of mine, the boss man. I bet you make a lot of dough. Got yourself a real nice setup."

"Look, you can stay here while we get to know one another, and you see some friends of mine. One is a nurse."

"I ain't seein' no nurse. I just came to see you and Mama Rose."

"Mama Rose? Have you spoken with her? Did you call her?"

"No, thought I would surprise her."

Chris looked him straight in the eye, like a cannon aimed at its target. "I don't think you should be bothering her, Jim."

"What do you mean bothering her? She's my mother."

"Well, there's something you should know about Mama Rose. She isn't the same."

"What do you mean not the same?"

"She doesn't know anyone, Jim. She has Alzheimer's disease."

Jim looked dazed.

"Twenty-five years is a long time, you know. A lot has happened."

"Yeah, guess so." His voice was almost a whisper.

"Well, I'm going to leave you now. Get some rest, and I'll pick you up in the morning."

Jim barely acknowledged Chris as he lay on the bed, his head propped up against the brass headboard, staring into space.

She shut the door behind her.

CHAPTER 4

Restoration Love

The following day Chris went to the office to answer some calls and catch up on emails before going to the hotel to pick up Jim. But the morning didn't go as planned. Admissions numbers were extremely high, the head of the adolescent unit wanted to speak with Chris, and the nurses' union called a meeting over vacation time.

"Shep," she said into the phone, "can you do a favor for me?"

"Sure," he said as he petted Riker on the head in the chapel office.

"Can you pick up Jim while I meet with the union negotiator this morning?"

"I would be glad to. How did it go when you picked up Jim yesterday?"

"Well, not like you might think. There were no apologies, signs of remorse, or questions about my life. He seems solely focused on himself. Listen, thanks for picking him up. Just bring him to your office, and I'll come by and get him from there."

"Will do, Chris. No worries. Riker and I have it covered."

As he hung up the phone, he looked at Riker and said, "Let's go pick up Mr. Jim Warren." He scooped up the keys to his truck, and Riker happily followed. They left the chapel through the rose garden.

Shep noticed a patient sitting on a bench outside. He approached with care, seeing her hospital bracelet. "Good morning. How are you today? My name is Shep." Shep and Riker walked closer.

"I am fine," the brown-haired girl said quietly. "I am Olivia."

"Nice to meet you." Shep extended his hand. "Riker, meet Olivia. Give her a solid paw shake, now."

"I like dogs." Olivia petted Riker's head and smiled slightly.

"Well, he is a pretty good sidekick. As the chaplain here at Hopewell Hill, I like to visit the patients, and sometimes I bring Riker along—if that suits you."

"Sure, I guess."

"Well, we'll see you soon then. We're off on an errand. Enjoy the garden and the sunshine. I see green leaves on those roses. Spring is on its way."

At the Crown Hotel, Riker followed Shep to the front desk. "I'm here to pick up a guest of yours. His name is Jim Warren."

"Uh, I think he's over there," the front desk attendant said as her face strained. She pointed to the game table.

Shep glanced across the room toward the card table in the corner. Two men were seated there, a naïve-looking bellboy and a grizzled old-timer with a scowl on his face—undoubtedly Jim. Shep walked over to the table as the bellboy laid down his cards.

"A royal flush?"

"I ... I can't help the cards I got," the bellboy said.

"Either you're cheating, the cards weren't shuffled, or you've got a rabbit's foot in your pocket, 'cause no one gets a royal flush just like that," Jim said.

"I gotta go help out in the back now." Glancing up with a frightened look at Shep, the bellboy quickly removed himself.

As Jim picked up the cards in a huff, Shep extended his firm hand. "Hi, my name is Shep. Do you happen to be Jim Warren?"

"That's my name." Jim didn't bother to look up while retrieving his poker chips.

"I'm here to give you a lift to the hospital today. Your daughter sent me."

Jim shot a stare from the table. "What? A Rock Hudson kind of priest and a dog? You wouldn't catch me dead goin' with a preacher and a dog anywhere, not even to my funeral." Jim laughed at his joke with haughty glee.

"Oh, the white collar. Yes, guess I forgot I had this on. I'm the hospital chaplain at Hopewell Hill, where Chris works.

I wear this so the patients will know who I am when I make rounds." Shep pulled the collar off and loosened the neck of his shirt. "Chris is busy this morning and asked me to come for you. This here is my dog Riker."

"Riker, huh? Well, not a bad-looking dog, I guess." Riker panted back at Jim. "Not happy about this. I thought Chris was picking me up."

He shuffled his cards into a neat pile, gathered his chips, and put them into his poker tin. The graphic of cards and gambling chips on the lid had faded. "But guess I'll have to go with you, seeing that's the only way." Jim's brow furrowed as he reconsidered his options. "Wait. How far to walk from here? Before leaving this deadbeat town, I need to talk with my daughter again."

"Well, if you walked there, it could take over an hour. Riker won't be any trouble. He'll hop in the back of my truck. Let's go," Shep said with authority.

Jim stood up, walked toward the front desk favoring his right leg, and asked the desk clerk to put his beat-up poker box in his room. Then he followed Shep outside.

Riker ran to the truck.

"In the back, ole boy." The Border collie obeyed without hesitation, and when Shep unlatched the hitches and put the tailgate down, Riker hopped up. "It's been a long winter, but finally warm enough for you to ride in the back," he said as he rubbed Riker's head and slammed the tailgate shut.

Jim stood dumbfounded when he saw the antique truck. Slowly he began walking around to the hood section. "I used to have a Ford, but I was a teenage boy the last time I saw one of these oldies."

"I found her rusted, dilapidated, and the inside rotted out," Shep said.

The meadow-green 1951 Ford Woody truck gleamed in the sun. The wax job revealed the beauty of a bygone time. A massive rolling hood with blinker lights sitting high on the fenders, with a grill that was a work of art and vents inset in the hood for air intake. A large steel bar linked the headlights. Silver letters proudly spaced spelled F O R D on the front.

Jim admired the artistry while running his hands over the smooth painted finish of the protruding fender flares. The side mirrors were vintage-like, and the door handles pulled straight down. As Jim walked toward the back, Riker met him, panting and wagging his head over the wood gating pieces fitted into the sides, finished in wood stain perfection. The outside hitches that Shep had used to unlatch the tailgate were utterly old school. The muted green paint of the logo on the wooden tailgate subtly displayed F O R D. This automobile was a lesson in restoration love.

Jim drew himself together. "Well, guess there is no hiding when a preacher man comes around in this."

Shep said, "No, guess not."

Jim opened the door and slid into the brown leather seat. The steering wheel was large and thin and showed wear from where Shep and owners before him had driven it. The steel stick shift had a black ball for the shifter.

Jim took Skoal out of his pocket and dipped some with his finger. He lodged it back into the left side of his mouth.

Miniature boxing gloves with tiny letters on each glove hung from the rearview mirror, just like a small pair of dice.

"A pair of gloves." Jim motioned his head toward them. "I used to box."

"Oh, you did? I'm a crusty old guy from the ring too." Shep touched the gloves, and when he did, the words *God's* on one glove and *Love* on the other showed.

With a satirical laugh, Jim said, "Yeah, that's how God's love is, all right. He punches you down in life, and he keeps punchin' and punchin' till the big ref in the sky calls OUT!"

"It's a matter of how you look at it. Some would say God's love is the best way to fight the battles in your life. You will always come out victorious." Shep started the engine and put the truck in drive.

"You preacher types, all the same, talk all your gobbledygook. Let's just go to this hospital place. I need to see my daughter before I leave here."

As they left the parking lot, Shep said, "This old truck was a lifesaver for me. Getting out of prison and settling in Hopewell, it gave me a project to focus on. I kept seeing it on my way to my job at the hospital. It was in this man's front yard, just wasting away. One day, I finally got the nerve to stop and ask the owner if he would sell the rusty heap. To my surprise, he was willing to give it away. He said it was useless to him. It was in such bad shape I had to get a flatbed and tow it home. My wife, Annie, who was sick then, wasn't thrilled with that hunk of junk in our driveway." Shep chuckled.

"You were in the tinker and married? Are you sure you're a preacher?"

"Chaplain, and, yes, I am sure." Shep rolled his window down and smiled. "I thought everything would be so much better when I got home from prison. But time wasn't on our side. She was so young, only thirty-two. We were just kids when we fell in love. Then there was my prison time. So our time together was short after I got out and came home."

Silence hung between them.

Jim sighed. "I always say hard things make you a man. You can't let anything drag you down. Got to be the last man standing."

"Is that how you feel, Jim? Like the last man standing?"

"Maybe. Maybe."

After leaving the Crown Hotel, they drove through the town of Hopewell. This understated borough was full of a quiet life. Coffee shops and bistros sat next to antique shops and the hardware store. Next to the drugstore with its mortar and pestle graphic, Shep turned right off Main Street. Cruising through the March wind in the Ford, windows down, they made their way down a winding country road. Winter was thawing, and buds were on the trees.

The terrain continued upward, both sides of the road dotted with evergreens. As they came to a stop, the old truck blinker tinked to turn left into the hospital entrance. A Hopewell Hill sign, needing a bit of repair, creaked in the wind.

"Where the heck are we?"

"At an older yet refined mental health hospital," Shep said. "Your daughter is one reason why patients receive such good care here."

"Well, it ain't no place for me."

CHAPTER 5

Sacred Spaces

They weaved through the property, around the Hill School, the main hospital, and older buildings needing repair to the far corner of the grounds. Shep parked his truck in the parking lot behind the chapel.

"Chris said she would catch up with you here, Jim, in my office."

"What kind of office is this, anyway?" Jim asked.

"This is the chapel and my office, which sit adjacent to the hospital. Let's go to the front so you can get a proper entrance."

Jim stepped out, smoothed out what hair he had left, tucked in his shirt, and repositioned his blue jeans with a tug of his belt before following Shep.

They proceeded on the small stone path through the rose garden. Jim's boots crunched the gravel as he followed Shep. The smell of nearby pine trees wafted freshly into the air. Peacocks in the side yard fluttered and cooed at the sight of them, fanning their blue, purple, and taupe feathers as they ran in the opposite direction.

"Here she is. Welcome to Grace Chapel." Tan and white stone blended into a welcoming wood porch and hewn-timber steps. Three arched windows on each side of the church displayed colorful stained glass, and a bell tower stood atop the structure with a cross on the top. The steps rose to an arched red door.

Jim gazed up at the chapel. "Sure looks old."

"It is. We believe a group of farmers built it, and it served the community for decades. Eventually, the hospital bought all the surrounding farmland."

Over the doorway in wooden letters, it read:

GRACE CHAPEL
Est. circa 1812

Shep opened the door with its arrow-shaped hinges. "Come on in."

Jim looked a little pale but smiled briefly and stepped in. Riker followed.

Four church pews of mahogany were on the left and four on the right of the center aisle. In the front, at the altar, was a large stained-glass pictorial. The cross in the center was made of wood and looked quite old. Behind it, jags of orange, red, violet, yellow, green, and blue glass had formed an arch around it to make up the background. The light from the sun began to break through the cloudy morning, pouring in through the stained-glass windows.

Jim walked slowly up the stone floor aisle toward the front altar. He touched the pews with engraved initials and names that somebody had notched in them. Slogans like *S. H. loves Ben* and a heart with the initials *J. D.* inside it were just a few. The graffiti seemed to only add to the chapel's beauty.

"The students from our Hill School helped me restore this." Shep pointed to the stained-glass centerpiece. "This old cross was always part of this chapel. I thought it would be nice, when the glass around it needed to be replaced, to have the kids take part in fixing it. So I asked several kids who attended my youth group meetings to select their favorite glass color. Then I worked with each one individually to break their glass into a shape they liked. We smoothed some of the edges and then pieced them into the background. The kids did a great job and loved participating in this project. I remind them that God loves who they are individually, just like these shapes. In their brokenness, they can become strong when surrounded by the cross."

"I always say stuff like that toughens up a kid. It truly is a work of art, though." Jim walked over to a pedestal near the altar. He touched a wooden book lying there. The front panel of the book was made of rich, deep tones of cherry wood and had the letters *H O P E* intricately carved with swirls on it.

"I used to do woodworking a long time ago." Jim ran his fingers across the front.

"Oh, you did? Did you have chisels and gouge tools?"

"I did until I lost them in a card game. I used to enjoy working with my hands."

"What did you make?"

"Chairs, tables, chests. That sort of thing."

"Creating furniture takes a skilled craftsman."

"I guess it passes some time."

"Then you can appreciate the kind of work this book entails. One of our former patients made this *H O P E* book with the help of Hector from maintenance. They carved the letters on the front and put the hinges on it to form this large book so that other patients could leave notes of encouragement in their healing time here at Hopewell Hill. Your daughter encourages patients to do works of art like this and write letters of recovery so they can help others as well."

"Really? My Chris?"

"Yes, your Chris."

Jim stood looking a bit bewildered. His hands were shaky as he looked at some of the patients' letters.

Shep let Jim peruse the book before asking, "Do you want to join Riker and me in my office for tea while we wait for Chris?"

"Sure, I guess."

Shep led the way through a breezeway from the left of the altar. He unlocked the door to his office. "Come, have a seat. Either chair you like. I'll start a fire to knock off this March chill."

The chapel office was small with hewn wood log walls butting up to the stone fireplace. Glossy wood plank floors ran under a colorful brown-and-purple braided rug. Shep's desk sat at one end, near a window that looked out to a field that would soon turn green. A paperweight that said *FORD* sat on top of some files, and a well-worn Bible sat on his desk.

Jim sat in one of the leather wingback chairs, and Riker sat beside him.

Shep started the tea kettle on his kitchenette stove. "Black tea fine?"

"Sure. Not accustomed to having tea with a preacher."

"Well, it's been a long time since I have had someone from out west in my office. Tell me about your mountains out there."

The two settled in, with Riker resting in between, for a fireside chat that warmed more than fingers and toes.

CHAPTER 6

Daydreams

Chris and Jim walked into the Shady Brook nursing home. "This might be a quick visit."

"It might be, but surely Mama will recognize me, her son."

They checked in at the front desk. Chris said hello to several nurses who knew her from all the times she had visited her grandmother.

Jim rubbed the back of his neck before straightening his shirt. "I want to go in first and see her alone. Let's see if she knows me without anyone else around."

"Well, um, okay. I don't know if that is a good idea, but I'll be here if you need me." Chris hesitated, then sat down in one of the familiar green waiting chairs. The attendant showed Jim to his mother's room. Chris watched Jim fade down the hallway. He once had a swagger, but now he had a slight limp. She pulled back her hair and cleared her throat as she turned to look out the window. Outside, sprouting tulips were not yet showing their blossoms. Weathering themselves against the wind, they bent and blew. Chris felt the same way after these last few days. She tried to be hopeful but braced herself for another disappointing chill from this man called Jim Warren. If only an actual springtime could arise in their lives.

Chris gazed out to the grassy yard, remembering that after she and Helen moved to New Jersey and Jim was no longer in their lives, she made up ideas about who her father was. As she spent time in her bedroom playing records and daydreaming, Chris imagined that Jim was an excellent outdoorsman, probably because he really was. Still, she fantasized that people requested Jim to take them on big hunting and fishing excursions because of his hunting skills. He would take Chris on one of his fishing trips, and as they were together, he would tell her stories and show her beautiful landscapes and rivers. They would catch the best fish and wade in beautiful rivers as they cast their lines over sun-drenched rapids. All the while, they would be laughing, talking, and enjoying each other.

Suddenly, Jim stood before her. He gave out a long, slow sigh.

Startled, Chris asked. "Well, how did it go?"

"I guess too many years have passed. She didn't even know who I was."

"Really?" Chris tried to act surprised. "I'm sorry. She waited for you to come home, but the disease has progressed."

"Yeah, sometimes a man just tries to get his horse ready for the rodeo, but by the time he thinks he has it all trained up, the rodeo has already left town." Jim slumped into the chair next to Chris.

"I'll go back and say hello to her for a minute. Just wait here."

As Chris walked toward her grandmother's room, she couldn't help but think how long her grandmother had waited for this day.

Chris tapped gently on room 311 and then opened the door. Grandma Rose sat in her reclining chair in the corner. "Hi, Rose. It's me, Chris."

Rose wore a pink-and-purple flowered duster with house shoes to match. Her hair was white, and her fuchsia lipstick stood out from her wrinkled skin.

"Oh, hello. Nice to meet you. Chris? Did you say? Today must be my lucky day. I am getting so many visitors. Did you know a cowboy just visited me? He had a silver belt buckle. I thought he was handsome, so I colored my lips in case he returned." Rose chuckled, shrugged, and gave Chris a wink.

Chris's heart sank as she looked at Rose and then around the room. The room she helped set up the day she and Helen moved Grandma Rose to Shady Brook. They made sure her small bedroom had all the comforts of home. They put her favorite quilt, made of white and lemon yellow with purple lilacs on each square, on her twin maple bed. The small matching dresser had a crocheted doily on top, and her mirror above had pictures of loved ones stuck inside the frame. Chris looked down at the red-and-brown rug on the floor beside her bed. She had made sure it came to Shady Brook with Grandma Rose.

Chris smiled and tried not to show her disappointment. "Oh, that's nice. Did you have a good lunch today?"

Rose began recounting. "Oh, it was a lovely lunch. Momma and Daddy were there, of course. Everything was from the garden: fresh tomatoes, new potatoes, and greens. Of course, Momma had the table set beautifully with her china. It was perfect. I must say I am a little tired. It was such a big day."

Almost as soon as Rose finished recalling this long-ago memory, she began dozing off. Chris was disappointed, but she was familiar with Grandma Rose's ways now.

Thinking of Sunday dinners from long ago made Chris remember all those Grandma Rose had hosted for her and Helen. At one of those dinners, Rose pulled Chris aside and said, "You know, I had an interesting thing happen to me. I was sitting here reading in my bed this morning, and I just got so overcome with worry about your father, about Jim. So, I got down here to pray on my rug where I always do."

The little red-and-brown braided rug lay on the floor beside her bed. It was worn in the center by grandmother, who had knelt on it for so long. The indentations in the prayer rug had a comfortable look, just like when you put on a soft house shoe that fits your worn-out feet perfectly. There was comfort and holiness to this little rug. It was hallowed ground.

Grandmother said, "Before I knelt, I felt my hands. They seemed so rough and dry, I reached for my lotion and rubbed some on. My hands felt better. Then I opened my Bible and found these words from Jeremiah 32:27: 'Is anything too hard for me?' I felt like God was saying to me, 'Don't worry. Nothing is too hard for me. I can heal hearts and hands.' I know God can find Jim and bring him home to us."

Chris hugged her grandmother tight that day. She could see how distraught she had been over Jim and his gambling life. He was her wayward child, her little lost sheep.

Chris blinked and looked at her grandmother, who was still fast asleep. She walked over and gently kissed her on the forehead. "Rest now, Grandmother. It's been a big day. Cowboys and all." She quietly shut her door and let the nurses know she had left her sleeping.

Jim was quiet as they walked to the car and looked down at the ground. He had a book in his hand.

"What do you have there?"

"The ole girl still is a Bible-toting believer; she gave me one of her good books. She has several, you know."

"I'm glad she did."

They sat in silence in the car on the ride to the hotel. Like a child, Jim stared out the passenger window, looking up at the trees as they drove.

Looking at Jim beside her, she realized how different he was from her dreams. Remembering her teenage fantasy that Jim was a successful businessman who knocked on the front door one day and looked so handsome as he smiled and said, "I'm here now. Let's start over, and let me show you the best of everything—a lovely home, the best of schools, and travel to exciting places." He was handsome, dressed in a well-made suit, and smelled of expensive cologne. He hugged her, and she felt loved and secure in his strong arms.

Chris parked in front of the Crown Hotel. "Shep has agreed to pick you up in the morning. I know today may have been a little much for you, so tomorrow, Shep wants to show you some things around town."

"Okay, I guess so." He got out of the car, seemingly still lost in his thoughts.

Chris rolled down the window. "Don't forget this."

Jim leaned down and peered through the window opening.

As Chris handed the Bible over to him, a few one-hundred-dollar bills slid out. She slipped them back in without a word and handed the book to Jim while squinting at him disapprovingly. Remembering how her grandmother kept cash in her Bible, she was sure Jim had recalled her stashing secret and willingly took the book.

"I'm sure you will need this and the contents thereof."

He grabbed the Bible from her hands. "Oh, yes! Indeed." He mockingly patted it, like an unfavored pet.

"Good night, Jim. I hope we get some time to sit down and talk this weekend and get to know each other when things aren't so hectic at the hospital. I want to give you some pictures. Wait a minute." She looked around in her leather bag. "I have them right here in an envelope. I was trying to address this to you but wasn't sure where to send it. These are some pictures of you and me that Mom took when I was little."

He took the envelope and pulled out a picture of Chris when she was three. Soft ringlet curls circled her baby tear-streaked face as she sat on Jim's knee.

"I remember this time. That photographer sure scared you. Helen and I couldn't get you to stop crying."

He looked at another one, this one a rare family portrait. "There's Helen. How's the tough old broad, anyway? Is she married?"

"Yes, she remarried about twenty years ago. She's happy. She married a pastor."

"Ha, figures. Preachers are coming out of the woodwork around here."

"Jim, she's made of steel, with a heart of gold. We were able to start a new life here."

"Guess you're right." Jim looked at the ground and then thumped the car door. "Well, see you around, kid. You did okay without your old man, anyway."

Jim walked away with shoulders slumped. He looked wounded by his losses from today and all his yesterdays.

Chris had her losses too. Heart losses. Wounds of a void relationship, torn open and bloodied again. Tears forming, she drove away as a soft rain began to bead on the windshield.

Thinking back through the day between Grandma Rose and Jim, she could see how the years had flown by and changed everything. Like sheets of paper carelessly tossed by the wind from a calendar, the best years of their lives seemed gone.

Just then, a black cat ran in front of the car, and Chris slammed on the brakes. The soaked kitten scampered into the woods. Saying a few choice words to the cat out loud, Chris put her head on the steering wheel. Then she whispered, "How could you not love me, your daughter? Why have you stayed away for so long? All the years of wondering if you were homeless or somewhere in prison. God, why did he do this to us?"

The motion of the windshield wipers back and forth couldn't hum away her sobs. Eventually, Chris took a deep breath and adjusted the rearview mirror until her face came into view. She wiped the smeared mascara under her green eyes and smoothed out her streaked foundation. In a few minutes, she straightened the mirror and put her hands on the steering wheel.

"Well, Grandma Rose, one thing is for sure: your little sheep has finally found his way home, but he sure is lost."

CHAPTER 7

Birdsong

"Hey, Shep, let me walk with you." Sharon jogged to catch up to Shep. "Are you on your way to the adult unit?"

"Hi, Sharon. If it isn't my favorite nurse. Yes, I'm headed there to do some patient rounds. Come join me." They walked together past the stone fountain spewing water in front of admissions. The sun was shining, and the buds on the saucer magnolias were about to bloom.

"How are things, Shep? I've heard you've been busy with a newcomer in town."

"Me? Oh, have you been talking to Chris?"

"Yes, she let me know about her dad. Sounds like he is one tough customer."

"Well, that might be one way of describing him."

"I feel for her. How is she going to manage all this? You know she runs a tight ship here, and her plate is full, and now this. I had no idea she had a gambling dad. Gee, she always has it so together. I never would have known that. You never know what kind of parents people have."

"It's true, Sharon. You never do. We have to do the best with what we have. Sometimes we wish parents could give more than they really can."

"Speaking of parents, there is a new patient, Olivia, that I want you to stop and see. Her parents are very concerned about her."

Shep looked at his rounding sheet from the front office, a list of patients who had requested a chaplain visit. "Olivia? She was recently admitted?"

"Yes."

"Here she is. I see her name now. I met her briefly in the rose garden."

"Good. I'm sure she'll benefit from an in-room visit from you. The first twenty-four hours were tough for her, but the worst is now over. She's on meds now, and we'll see where we go from here. The parents wanted to make sure you visited. I do my nurse thing, but you, Shep, are like disaster relief showing up after an EF5 tornado. Also, on another note, Chris has asked us to go over to Jim's hotel together so I can do an assessment of him if he's willing, and that's a big if. See you in the morning."

"Okay, I'll see you then."

The two parted ways at Olivia's room.

Shep knocked softly on the varnished door of room 28. "May I come in?"

"Yes," Olivia answered.

Quietly, Shep entered. Pale-blue walls gave calm to the room. A large window displayed a cherry tree about to bud in the courtyard outside. The lamp by the bed gave off soft lighting that took the edge off the hospital fluorescents. Shep put his hand out to greet her. "Hello, Olivia. I'm Shep, the hospital chaplain. Do you mind if I come in for a little visit?"

"I guess it's fine."

"Do you recall we met the other day in the rose garden?"

"Oh, yes, I remember." She forced a smile. Her straggly, light-brown hair fell softly around her round freckled face. There was little color in her cheeks. As she shook hands softly with Shep, a picture she held fell on the crisp, starched sheets.

"Are you feeling a little better?"

"I've had a hard few days, but yes, feeling better."

"May I ask whose picture you brought with you?" Shep nodded toward the photo.

"I don't mind. It's my boyfriend, Allen." Olivia showed Shep the picture.

"Oh, he is one handsome fella." A blond-haired young man in blue jeans and a white T-shirt stood smiling in front of a riverbank. "Have you been dating a long time?"

"We have. He has always been there for me. I wish I could be there for him."

Shep sat on the chair beside her bed and the window. "I feel sure you will be able to do that. With the resolve I hear in your voice and the excellent doctors and nurses here at Hopewell Hill, everyone wants to see you get well very soon."

Olivia smiled at Shep with a little stronger smile than before.

"Oh, I see you have a window by the bird feeder." Amber-breasted robins and an occasional blue jay pecked at the seed that had fallen on the ground. The birds' chirping was muffled by the glass. "Did you know there are over ten thousand species of birds in the world?"

"I haven't paid much attention."

"Each one of them has a different sound and coloring. Kind of like us—everyone has their unique look and personality. Sometimes I think about how we are more varied than all the birds in the world." Shep turned to look at Olivia. "May I tell you a little story about a conversation between two songbirds?"

"Well, yes, I guess."

Shep paused and then looked outside at the grass and trees. "It goes like this:

"One little bird chirped to the other, 'What is the greatest love song of all?' The robin turned his head one way and then to the other and answered."

———

There is no sweeter sonnet than the one
God sings to me
I love to hear his voice on lonely branch or tree
His Spirit gently guides me to each windowsill
So I may sing sweet notes for others or just be still
I know my maker loves me. He caused me to fly
And when I am with Him, he hears each
chirp and cry
All I have to do is trust Him. He is so very dear
Then I can be courageous and soar without fear
He is my heavenly Father, and He touches
my little bird soul
He cares for me daily when life takes its toll
I never have to worry because I know
He is always here
My heavenly Father,
Listening, loving me, and drawing me near.

A tear ran down Olivia's cheek. "I never thought of birds in that way."

"We are all God's creatures, Olivia. Maybe, as you look out your window watching the birds, you can ponder that and realize you are very special to God too. He loves you and wants to see you get well."

Just then, the intercom system blared from the hallway. "Shep to administration. Shep to administration."

"Well, I hear I am being paged. That intercom is a bird of another type. I'll come again and bring along my friend you have already met, Riker, next time. The birds might scatter when they see him through the window."

"Thank you for coming."

"Until next time." Shep cupped her hand in his and said goodbye.

CHAPTER 8

In the Ring

Shep and Sharon drove their cars to the hotel separately.

"I'll go in and introduce myself and get started with Jim. You can wait here until I'm finished and then take him on your tour of the town, Shep."

"Okay. I hope Mr. Jim Warren complies."

"Well, let's hope he does. Like Chris says, she has to start intervening at some point."

Sharon knocked on Jim's room door. "May I come in? It's Sharon from Hopewell Hill. Your daughter sent me over."

Jim opened the door. "I thought that preacher was picking me up this morning."

"Oh, he is. He is waiting outside. I'm here because your daughter wanted me to check in with you. Is that okay?"

"Well, all right." Jim sat down.

Sharon set her bag down and took out her blood pressure cuff. "So, you are Jim Warren."

"Yeah, that's what they call me, but I've been called worse," Jim said.

"I'm a nurse, a friend of your daughter's. Chris asked me to do an initial assessment with you today. Is that okay with you?"

"You can visit with me all you want, but if you think you're going to lock me up in some cuckoo ward, you got another think comin'."

Sharon slowly said, "No, Mr. Warren, this is totally on my own time and not officially with the hospital. I'll just take your vitals and ask some initial questions."

"I just agreed to a talk today, not get poked!"

"This will just take a minute, and no poking involved." Sharon stared over her tiger-striped readers as her blondish curls edged her face. She pulled a blood pressure instrument out of her medical bag.

Jim reluctantly lifted his arm with a huff.

"Okay, Mr. Warren, I am just going to take your blood pressure," Sharon said as she wrapped the Velcro band around his arm.

"I ain't agreed to nothin', but go ahead and let's see how much you nurse types get my blood pressure up."

Sharon watched the meter as she started pumping. She swallowed hard. "Uh, Mr. Warren, take some deep breaths and try to relax, and let's get another reading."

She pumped again, 160/89. "Your blood pressure is high."

"I don't know what you're talking about. You got a faulty machine there." Jim scooted around in his chair.

"Faulty machine?" Sharon said. "Mr. Warren, nothing is faulty about this machine, but an old cowboy like you might want to wake up and realize you could be near a stroke or heart attack with a blood pressure reading like this. If you don't want to visit that prairie in the sky anytime soon, I suggest you see a doctor and possibly get on some medication."

Jim chuckled and smiled his Santa Claus smile. It was as if Sharon had played her poker hand with Jim and won the first round.

"I've gotten along this far without no doc. I'll make it some more."

"Well, I will document this, and after you spend some time here over the next few weeks, we can order a full physical."

"Look, I'm not one of your monkeys! Leave me alone!"

"Mr. Warren, your daughter only asked me to come and check on you because she's concerned for your welfare. Let's calm down a minute." Sharon wrapped the blood pressure cuff and instrument back up and put them into her bag.

"So, Mr. Warren, Chris tells me that gambling is your hobby?"

"Hobby? Hobby? That's how I make my livin'. I hardly call it a hobby."

"Okay," Sharon said. "Mr. Warren, let me ask you a couple of questions. Have you lost time from work due to gambling?"

"What? When I want to work, I do. That's it."

"Has gambling affected your reputation?"

"My reputation is intact: don't mess with Jim."

"Have you ever gambled until your last dollar was gone?"

"If it weren't for those inept card dealers, I wouldn't be sitting with you here and now!"

"Okay, Mr. Warren, I have just asked you a few questions from Gamblers Anonymous to assess if you may have a gambling problem. I think you may need help."[1]

"I think you are out of your mind. Show yourself out, little lady, and tell that preacher I'll be down in a minute. Riding with him has got to be better than sittin' here being interrogated by you."

"All right, Mr. Warren. Just know your daughter cares about you. She is only trying to help."

"I don't need any help."

---

1   "20 Questions: Are You a Compulsive Gambler?"
     Gamblers Anonymous, accessed April 11, 2024, https://
     www.gamblersanonymous.org/ga/content/20-questions.

Exhaust could be seen from Shep's truck as he sat idling. "You've got yourself a fun time today, Shep," Sharon said as she opened the door of her car, parked next to Shep's. "Have at it. He's a piece of work. I'll see you back at the hill."

"Oh boy, thanks for the warning."

Jim exited the hotel with his duffel bag hanging low to conceal it from Shep. Jim put the duffel softly into the back of the truck. Riker came over to greet Jim and sniff the bag. Riker looked at Jim and cocked his head sideways. "There, now, no questions from you," Jim whispered, patting Riker's black-and-white head. He hopped into Shep's truck. "Let's get out of here. That nurse has my blood pressure up. Where are we going today?"

"Hi, Jim. I thought we might see some friends of mine at the airport."

"Airport? Are you some kind of pilot?" Jim scoffed.

"Well, actually, not yet, but I've been taking flying lessons from a friend named Cal."

"Cal? Is that his real name?"

"No. My friend is pretty darn smart, good at calculus and science, so some buddies and I nicknamed him Cal. He's the best pilot in town, and I would fly between any mountain with him to land on a dime." Soon they turned onto the road leading to the regional airport. "Cal will meet us at Pete's place, in the hangar next door. Pete has something more than an airplane to show you."

When they reached the hangar, Shep beat his fist against the metal door. "You in there, Pete?"

"Comin', I'm coming!" Pete answered. The hangar door pulled open with a loud rattle. A bent-over older man appeared with a faded green Philadelphia Eagles baseball cap and a weathered face but smiled when he saw Shep and gave him a big hug and pat on the back.

"Well, if it isn't my old friend Shepherd! Glad to see you." He clasped Shep's forearm and looked into his eyes. "What brings you here today?"

"I want you to meet a new friend of mine. This is Jim," Shep said.

Pete shook Jim's hand and said, "Pleased to meet you. You, sir, are in good company."

Jim half smiled.

"Come on inside. Coffee is over there." Pete shuffled toward his office.

"What is that?" Jim looked toward the back of the hangar, empty of a plane. In full size, there was a boxing ring with a mat, ropes, and a punching bag near it.

"No airplane in here. You're looking at Pete's boxing ring. After he stopped flying, he built this ring. All the local pilots, doctors, and boxing trainers know about it. Pete used to be a big-league boxing manager in the heavyweight circuit."

"That old guy?"

"Yes, that old guy. You mentioned you liked boxing, so I thought you would enjoy seeing this."

"You're right. I didn't think I would see a ring today." Jim walked over and grabbed the rope around the edge of the ring. As he walked the length of the boxing mat, he ran his hand along the cord.

Shep watched him as he made small talk with Pete.

"Care for a round in the ring, preacher?" Jim put up his dukes.

"Oh, I don't think so."

Jim took his shoes off and climbed into the ring, holes in his gray wool socks.

"Well, are you sure?"

"If you insist." Shep took off his watch, then his leather jacket. With a wary eye on Jim, he slipped off his shoes.

Jim bounced around the ring with gloves on, punching around.

"Just for a warm-up." Shep ducked his muscular frame under the rope and into the ring.

Jim punched the air with his black gloves. He began to spar off from Shep's red ones.

The pair danced around the mat. Pete looked up from reading his newspaper.

"You know, I used to knock some fellas out," Jim said as he punched a righty and a lefty into the air.

"I'm sure you did."

Jim swung at Shep as they narrowed their focus closer to each other. Then Jim punched Shep's right cheek, and Shep stumbled back.

"You, you probably shouldn't be boxing with that preacher man, you know," Pete yelled from the corner.

"Looks like he can take it. Or maybe the preacher isn't as tough as he thinks he is," Jim huffed as he bounced around in his holey socks.

"Why do you like fighting, Jim? Fighting through life?" Shep whispered, with gloves up near his face in defense.

"Every man has to make his own way in life. Nobody ever helped me." He took a hard swing at Shep, releasing venom.

Shep stumbled backward, his face bleeding from the hit. Jim kept bouncing and laughing. Shep moved toward Jim again and whispered to him through his boxing gloves, "Jim, Jim the Struggler—that's your name. You want to struggle with God, Chris, and yourself. Why not make peace?" Shep continued the boxing dance.

"Peace! I'll give you a piece, a piece of me!" Jim swung hard, and Shep saw it coming, so he made an undercut swing toward Jim's face. Jim jumped quickly to the side. Shep's red glove hit Jim's left shoulder with a loud pop, and Jim fell to the ground.

"I think you knocked my shoulder out!" Jim said. "You SOB preacher!"

"Okay, boys, men, that's enough for today." Pete hopped into the ring and threw them both towels. "Get your gloves off, go over, get some water, and settle down."

Jim held his shoulder close and hobbled out of the ring.

Shep took his gloves off and wiped his cheek with Pete's towel, blood staining it.

"Tried to tell ya, Jim. Shep has a powerful swing."

CHAPTER 9

Rib Shack

Riker sensed the action in the hangar and started barking and circling around Jim as Pete tended to his shoulder. Just like a good sheepdog, he was spinning around his injured lamb.

"Okay, let's get a Pete's special on your shoulder."

"What is that?" Jim asked Pete, still reeling in pain.

"It's a tight homemade sling."

Riker barked and circled some more. Jim stared at the dog while he let Pete work on him.

Shep was gathering his watch and jacket when the hangar door opened.

"If it isn't Cal! Good to see you, my friend," Shep said.

"What is all the barking and commotion going on over here? I saw your truck outside and figured you might be here."

Riker ran over to greet Cal.

"Okay, Riker, that's all we need from you now." Shep shooed him outside.

"He'll be fine in our little airport. Everyone knows Riker, and the taxiways are fenced," Cal said.

"Jim, I want you to meet my flight instructor and friend."

"Well, at least I can still use my right hand," Jim said as he shook Cal's hand.

"Okay, buddy, that tight sling should help matters. It's a good thing it's not dislocated. Keep the sling on for a week or so," Pete said.

"Could we go over and show Jim your fine plane, Cal?" Shep asked.

With a fast smile, he said, "Sure!"

Jim fumbled with his shoes and dignity and followed Shep and Cal.

"See you around, Pete," Shep yelled.

Pete waved from his office. "Till next time, Shep."

The Cessna 180 in Cal's hangar sat tilted upward, its nose in the air and the tail to the ground. The blue-and-white paint sparkled on the body of the aircraft. If the taildragger could talk, it would say, "Let's go flying. I'm ready to go!"

"You sure keep it clean," Shep said as they began to look closer.

Cal smiled with pride. He slid a stool over to the door.

"Here, Jim, look inside at the instrument panel."

Jim stepped up to look in.

He took in a maze of instruments and gauges. Instrument flips and switches made up the panel behind the yoke. The gray leather interior was in mint condition. Logbooks occupied the small copilot seat. Two additional seats in the rear made it a four-seater.

"Pretty compact inside," Jim said as he stepped down.

"Yes, it is, but it's all the space you need," Cal said.

"Is this Cessna what you're learning to fly?" Jim asked Shep.

"Yes, learning. Right now, I am an unofficial copilot."

"Shep was a big help when I took Dr. Wilson out to meet his other buddies on a hunting trip out west."

"Out west? Where did you take them?" Jim asked.

"It's a pretty remote area. The doctor and his friends hunt in the backwoods of the Sawtooth Mountains of Idaho. They like the big game hunting there, right, Shep?"

Shep nodded.

"Sawtooth? I know it well. I fish in Redfish Lake in August and early fall," Jim said.

"Oh, that's neat. Flying into some mountain airstrips can be tricky, but I enjoy the challenge," Cal said as he closed the door on his Cessna.

"Yes, it can be," Shep agreed. "But the trip is beautiful, and the mountains are spectacular."

"Well, any pilot that can land this hunk of metal in the middle of some mountain on a grass strip gets my respect."

"Well, Jim, I guess we better get going. The day is moving on, and we should move on too," Shep said.

Jim held his wounded shoulder close as the men shook hands. Shep rounded up Riker, and they were on their way.

"Jim, I thought you might be getting a little hungry. Do you like a pile of ribs with sweet barbeque sauce and corn bread?"

"Who doesn't like that? Sounds good."

Jim looked behind him at Riker slobbering in the wind in the truck bed with his tongue hanging out.

"Looks like your dog heard you too. Riker's mouth is watering." Jim's eyes twinkled. "Where did you get that dog anyway?"

"Now that's an interesting story. One day, while I was serving as chaplain at Trenton State Prison, some guards from Rikers Island were moving a prisoner to Trenton State in one of their vans. The story goes that a Border collie stray had given birth to a litter of pups in this van. The guards had relocated the little family of mom and pups, but one got left behind. The guards were as surprised as anyone when they escorted a prisoner off the van at Trenton State to find this little pup asleep on the floor. The Rikers officers didn't want to return to New York with him. So me, being the chaplain, kind of neutral, you know, I stepped in and said I would take him. I thought he could be therapy for some of the prisoners. We all named him Riker after his birthplace, and that's the slobbering, mouthwatering, barbeque-hungry beast you see behind you. He was lost, but now he is found."

Jim rolled his eyes. "Well, that is some story. I was never happier than when I flew out of my mamma's litter!" he said in his husky voice.

"Oh? How old were you when you left home?"

"A teenager. I waited to leave until my younger brother, Billy, got a little older because I was in charge. Our dad left it to me, the oldest, to take care of things when he walked out. I was nine years old."

"That must have been hard."

"Yeah, and Mom didn't take the split so great. She had these fits of crying. We lived in a tiny rental house that barely had running water. Mom taught school, but the salary wasn't much. One night, she was having one of her crying spells. It was cold. I went outside to get more wood to keep the coals hot in our fireplace. I bundled her up and sang to her through the night while my little brother was sleeping, until morning, until we both had to go to school."

"Jim, I'm sure your mother never forgot that. Never forgot what you did for her."

"Maybe, maybe not, but living in a little shack with a crying woman is no way to go through life. So I escaped, much like your little mutt there."

Shep pulled into the abandoned lot on the edge of the Delaware River, near a worn-down trailer parked adjacent to an abandoned button factory. Rib Shack was painted in fluorescent orange on the side of a silver trailer. At one time, this had been a place of industry, and people thrived here. But now it looked like a scene from an old black-and-white movie where the world has ended and only one guy is left. Tumbleweeds of trash rolled along the ground. Shattered glass and graffiti littered the factory. Weeds grew from the cracks in the concrete pavement.

"We are here," Shep said. "This is the Rib Shack. Best ribs around. Come on, let's get something to eat."

"Here? No offense, Preach, but this looks like an abandoned warehouse over there, and this here looks like a shack, not a restaurant."

"Just trust me," Shep said as he got out of the car.

Riker was barking and circling, smelling the waft.

CHAPTER 10

The Escape

*Down alongside the Delaware River by that old
button factory, there's a place near the Trenton
Makes what the World Takes bridge. They cookin'
out of a trailer down there. That guy down there
can smoke some ribs. Makes 'em so sweet. The
meat just
falls off the bone.*

The smell of the smoke coming out of the trailer was mouthwatering. Dancing with excitement at the smell, Riker jumped down. Shep looked at him. "Stay put. Don't get lost around here."

Shep grabbed his priest's collar like a weapon. "We might need this for security." He put it on over his shirt and under his jacket. Even though he wasn't Catholic, Shep wore it to help identify him to the patients of Hopewell Hill as the chaplain.

Hopefully, it could protect him at the Rib Shack with Trenton gang members.

He slammed the truck door shut. He and Jim walked toward the Rib Shack. Suddenly, two men dressed in leather and belt chains came from behind the trailer and faced them with knives. "Hey, what you doing here?" They looked at Shep and Jim, then back at each other.

"Hello, boys. I heard you've got some great ribs down here. We wanted to try them. We are a little early for dinner. Are we the first customers for the night?" Shep adjusted his collar.

They slowly put their knives into their holders next to their belt chains. "Well, yeah. Yeah, the first customers for the night." They moved like a pair of Dobermans guarding a gang.

Maybe the collar tranquilized them, or perhaps it was Shep's tall and sure stature. Shep and Jim followed the barbeque smoke down to a few old, splintered picnic tables, the kind with the benches attached. "Boys, this is real fine dining here along the riverbank," Shep said in jest.

Before sitting down, Shep poked his head into the trailer. The cook was busy moving around in the kitchen. "It sure smells good in here. We followed this scent from Hopewell."

When the cook looked up, a smile as wide as the river's bridge came across his face. "Why, Shep, what are you doing down here?"

"Why hello, Jason!" Shep was delighted to see the former chef from the Trenton State Prison. "I should have known you were the genius behind these famous ribs I've heard about!"

Jason stepped outside, wiping his hands on his white apron. He and Shep, two old friends, embraced and patted each other on the back.

The Doberman pair, ready to pounce just moments before, began to relax and sat down at Shep's table.

"I'll serve you up real quick. Just have a seat over here with these two guys." Jason motioned. He walked Shep and Jim over to the table where the men were sitting as Jason made introductions. "Here is my old preacher, boys. We nicknamed him Shep. These boys are Darnel and Jack."

"Pleased to meet you." Shep offered them a respectful nod and handshake as he slipped his legs inside the opening at the picnic table and sat down. "Meet my friend, Jim."

"I'll fix us all a plate. Be just a minute. A slab is coming off the smoker in nothing flat." Jason hurried into the little trailer to prepare the meal. As he worked, he went back and forth inside and out of the trailer, to the smoker, then back in the kitchen.

Shep struck up a conversation with Darnel and Jack. "Do you boys do any fishing over there?" He nodded toward the river. Soon Shep was laughing and talking with the pair.

Jim leaned over and muttered to Shep, "Is there anyone you don't know?"

"I'm always up to meeting new friends. It's peaceful here on the river, don't you think, Jim?"

"You must have yourself some very rosy glasses you look through. All I see around here is some trash by the riverbank."

"Maybe you're not looking close enough for the real beauty in life, Jim."

"I've looked close enough! I started my day out with a good working shoulder. Now it's in a sling."

Jason brought the ribs. The smell was smokey, and the deep brown sauce dripped from the bone. Shep bowed his head in prayer. "Lord, thank you for this great meal with welcoming friends Jason, Darnell, and Jack. Thank you that Jim is here with us, and I pray you will heal his shoulder real fast. Amen."

They began to eat.

Soon, Shep and Jason were getting caught up on the happenings around Trenton and reminiscing. "You know, Shep, I was so sorry to hear about your Annie. After all, you went through a lot for her, being falsely accused of killing that drunk maniac of a father she had. And your prison time and all. I know Annie loved you. So sorry you lost her, brother."

"Thank you, Jason. These last few years haven't been easy, but God has a way of making good out of bad situations, even though at the time, it may not seem like it. Just have to trust and wait."

"Now that's some kind of philosophy," Jim muttered to Darnell and Jack. "Glad I don't employ that at the poker table."

As the night grew on, others came to eat dinner—a place where gang members laid down their weapons and came to forget for just a little while. The river glistened aside a string of lights over the picnic tables, forming a tic-tac-toe trellis in the sky above them.

Some others came, and much to Shep's delight, a band started setting up their musical instruments. Before long, the guitarist, the bongo player, and a man with a harmonica were playing some tunes.

After Jason had served everyone and all seemed satisfied, he joined the band. He grabbed a mike that they plugged into the generator they had set up for the trailer. "Hey, everyone, so glad you all could come over to the Rib Shack tonight. As you know, this is a no-fight zone that I have here, and so I'm glad you all are here to enjoy some of our ribs and some music. So let's do it! But first, I want to welcome someone very special to me."

Shep looked around to see who Jason might be talking about. He recognized a few of the faces from the prison.

"This person means a lot to me. That is why I'm standing here tonight, smoking these fine ribs for you all and enjoying this beautiful night. See, he helped me dig out of the hole I got myself in. He brought me out of a pit. Before I got out of the slammer, I decided to turn my life around, and this man helped me do it. His name is Shep. That's how I know him. He showed me the way when I couldn't find it myself." Jason's voice cracked. "Shep's my man now, so no one mess with him tonight. Stand up, Shep. Let's give my old friend a hand."

Embarrassed, Shep rose to a half-stand and waved to the crowd of bikers, gang members, and former inmates.

"I got a little song I'd like to dedicate to him. Thank you, Shep, for coming tonight, ole friend, and for bringing Jim, a new friend, with you. I hope you will come back and see us many more times here at the Rib Shack. You are always welcome here, Shep. Here it goes."

The boys beat their hands on a rusty overturned trash can, and the others joined the beat. Jason started his rap in a whisper:

Shep, Shep Shep, Shepherd Shep, Shep, Shep
Shep, Shep Shep, Shepherd Shep, Shep, Shep

Shep, he is here for you and me.
Make sure we can really see.
True things in life that are to be.

In God's hand, in God's hand, in God's hand, in God's hand,
Even tho we're all in chains,

Shep, he's here to wipe the stains,
Bring back hope and life again.
In God's hand, in God's hand, in God's hand, in God's hand

Shep Shep, Shep, Shep Shepherd Shep,
Shep Shep, Shep, Shep Shepherd Shep.

Even tho we wander off,
Lost sheep, we all think we're tough,
Shep, he never knows no fear.
He will find you, bring you near.
For God's love, for God's love, for God's love,
Never, never let you go.
Know this 'cause Shep told me so.

Shep, Shep, Shep, Shep Shepherd Shep,
Shep, Shep, Shep, Shep Shepherd Shep.

The boys kept the beat as Jason shouted, "Thanks, Shep, for coming tonight!"

The band started the next jam, with the guitarist starting a Jimi Hendrix song. Jim got up and walked toward the river, around the grounds, to stretch his legs and dip some Skoal.

Soon, Shep was saying good night to Jason and the others. He looked toward the riverbank and didn't see Jim anymore. "Jason, have you seen Jim?"

"Oh, saw him talking to Darnel a few minutes ago."

Shep smelled trouble.

"Ok, Jason, well, it was great seeing you. We must be going." He wrapped up some rib bones for Riker and headed toward the truck to find Jim. Out of the corner of his eye, he saw a motorcycle speeding away. He ran toward it. "Jim, Jim, wait!" Doberman Darnel was speeding away on his Harley, and Jim was holding on with his good right arm, his duffel bag tied onto the back of the bike. Riker barked after them, but in a flash, they were out of sight.

CHAPTER 11

The Gift

Shep stood at Chris's office door as he knocked. "May I come in?"

Chris looked up at the grievous look on Shep's face.

"What's wrong?"

"It's Jim. I have something to tell you."

"What?"

"He's ... well, he's gone."

"Gone? Where? Back to the hotel?"

"No. I don't know."

"What do you mean, you don't know? Weren't you taking him around town yesterday?"

"Yes, I was. We did go out to the airport to see a couple of my friends and then on to ..." Shep sat in one of the chairs facing her desk.

"Where? On to where?"

"Trenton." Shep looked downcast.

"Trenton!" Chris screamed.

"Yes, but it was just to this little place to get some ribs."

"Ribs, in Trenton? And then what?"

"He met, uh, someone. An acquaintance of mine, Darnell."

"Okay ... then?"

"Then Jim ran off with Darnell, his bag and all. They sped away on Darnell's motorcycle."

Chris stared at Shep, her mouth open, her skin tone suddenly pale.

"I have my friend Jason on it now. He's tracking them. Don't worry. We'll get a lead on where he is, and I will bring him back. You can count on me to find him. Besides that, he probably doesn't have much money. He may need to come back here for help," Shep said.

"No, he has at least a few hundred dollars from his mother. For him, that's a start to a poker game."

Shep shook his head. "Well, I will find him. Chris, I'm so sorry."

"Just leave me alone right now. If you find Jim, then what? Shep? Then what? He is unwilling to let anyone help him face his addiction," Chris said in an irritated tone.

"Good night, Shep. Thanks ... I guess, for even taking him around yesterday."

"Good night." He turned away solemnly.

Chris got up from her desk and closed her office door. Thankfully, everyone in the offices near hers had already left for the day. She put her head down on her desk and began to weep. All her hopes flooded out.

She cried, "God, all I wanted Jim to do was love me."

She picked up the phone and dialed. "Mom, he's gone."

Chris began to tell her mother about the day, about Shep losing Jim. She had called her the day Jim was coming to town. Now, she had to say to her he was gone.

Her mother listened to Chris tell the whole story of Jim's arrival, his brash tone, his distasteful attitude of visiting Grandmother Rose, and taking a Bible with money stashed in it.

"Mom, I wanted you guys to connect while he was here, but he is so focused on himself. He just seems so separated from us, from life."

"Did he ever mention that I wrote to him a few times?"

"No. What do you mean wrote to Jim?"

"I wonder if he received the letters in the first place. Grandma Rose gave me a post office box she used to have for him. Maybe it was old, but I never had anything returned."

"Why didn't you tell me that, Mom?"

"You went through enough without a father around. I just thought I would update him on what a wonderful daughter you are. If I told you and he didn't respond to my letters, you would be disappointed again, so I didn't mention it. I'm sorry Jim is gone, Chris. I really am. You and Shep did all you could do at this point. He has his own mind and makes his own choices. Jim needs help, but maybe he isn't open to change yet. You did the best you could."

"I love you, Mom. I'll talk to you soon." She hung up the phone. Chris felt better, as she always did after speaking to her mom. She tried to tidy up some business on her desk. As she did, a scene of when she was twelve years old flashed before her.

Chris was in middle school. It was a snow day; the Hopewell schools had closed due to road conditions. Helen was home with Chris, one of the perks of being a teacher in the same school district.

"Would you like to walk to the mini mart on the corner in the snow to get some milk?" Helen asked.

"Okay!" Chris was happy to get this time with her mom to go out in the snow to walk and play.

It was a still, white morning. The snowflakes had padded the earth with a deep layer of softness, buffering noise. All they could hear was their snow boots crunching in the snow.

"Look, Mom, the snowflakes are hitting my face! And tongue!" Chris stuck her tongue out to catch the snow, laughing and giggling.

"Yes, I see." Helen stuck her tongue out too.

"Each snowflake is different, Mom!"

"Yes, they are as unique as you are."

As calm and quiet as the winter snow, peace took place in Chris's heart. She knew what it was to be loved, that day and many other days, by Helen. Chris contemplated that memory for a minute. She thought of the gift of herself that her mother had given her. Helen was always there for her.

Chris felt that if someone were to read her life story in a newspaper article, some events in her life, like the black type on the page, would stand out, but even more meaningful were the white spaces in her life, the times no one else would ever read about.

Helen listened to Chris. "This girl is bullying me at school" or "I will never make the debate team." And the coming-of-age times, like when Chris was learning to drive that old green Vega, a stick shift, and Helen shouted, "Chris, just drive it like a race car!"

All the lonely phone calls from college, and the sad I-just-broke-up-with-my-boyfriend calls. Yes, one could read in the *Hopewell News* about Chris's sports achievements through high school or making the honor roll. But it was the unpublished times that counted, the white space that mattered the most.

The disappointment of Jim leaving came back to the forefront of her mind. As Chris closed her desk drawer, she saw a little rock she kept beside her pens. It was a shiny black stone she often fiddled with while on a phone call. Chris put the black rock in her white worsted wool coat pocket and put it on, adjusting her hair over the collar. She switched off the lights and made her way down the empty corridor.

She opened her car door and frustratedly tossed her briefcase in. As she did, she glanced at Grace Chapel across the parking lot. The lights were on inside. With hands in her pockets, she walked toward the chapel. It was quiet. The second shifters in the hospital were well into their work for the night. Chris walked up the stairs to the chapel door and turned the knob. The arrow-shaped hinges on the old door pointed inward as she opened it.

There, amid the soft lighting, she could see Shep in one of the pews. Chris sat down in the back. She sat in silence.

Shep looked to the back of the chapel. "It's you, Chris."

"Yes, it's me."

He moved down some rows to sit in front of the one Chris was in, then turned around as he leaned his muscular forearm on the back of the pew to talk to her.

"I'm so sorry, Chris."

"Shep, it's okay," Chris said with a sigh. "It wasn't you. It's Jim. It's his attitude. He doesn't want to stay here. He would have left anyway. I called my mother and told her everything."

"What did she say?"

"Oh, she just listened," Chris said. "She understands. She knows Jim, knows his ways. You aren't married to someone for that long and not get it. But I was just thinking tonight about her lifetime of giving to me and what Jim gave me. Jim only ever gave me two things, except for life itself. Do you know what they were?

"No, what?"

"One was a Nancy Sinatra album. You know, the one with the song 'These Boots Are Made for Walkin'.'"

Shep began to whisper and sing as he beat the pew with his hand to form the drumbeat to the song.

Chris cocked her head, curls softly falling around her face, and said, "Really? But it is apropos, right? Since that's what Jim has just done—walked right out of my life."

Shep looked a little embarrassed as he wished the music in him had not taken over.

"What was the other thing Jim gave you?"

"A little black onyx rock."

"A rock?"

"Here it is."

Chris brought her fist out of her pocket. She held her palm straight out to expose the onyx stone in her fist. "This rock!" A tear streaked her face. "Can you believe it?"

Shep's face was pained.

"Jim must have bought it at one of those gas stations in the desert that sold different types of rocks and stale popcorn. He probably bought it on his way home from a gambling trip. I've kept it in my desk drawer all these years."

Shep was silent for a while. Then he asked, "Chris, may we do something ... may we go to the front and pray?"

Chris nodded. She removed her coat and blazer, revealing her silk blouse over her slightly freckled skin and delicate bone structure. The two approached the chapel altar and knelt to pray. Chris placed the stone on the altar. They looked at each other tenderly. Chris, with her soft complexion, and Shep, with his rough and chiseled features, had one thing in common. Heartache. They bowed their heads, and Shep put his hand on Chris's.

Shep prayed, "Father, you know our hearts. We are sad that Jim would leave after a twenty-five-year absence. We wanted to get to know him. We hoped for reconciliation for Jim and Chris, father and daughter. Please look upon this humble gift Jim gave Chris many years ago to symbolize how you can turn dark things into positive things in our lives. Turn away the black stones in the tombs of our hearts—stones of unforgiveness, grudges, and hurt. Turn away Jim's stones of pride, gambling, and rebellion. Take all these hurts and turn them into white stones, as only you can, stones of grace, healing, and forgiveness."

Chris's tears dropped like rain onto the old wooden altar they leaned on.

Shep leaned over the altar and grabbed a tissue box. He handed Chris a tissue and held a strand of hair out of the way while she wiped her tears.

Then Shep's demeanor changed. His head bowed again, and with a more robust, deeper voice, he said, "Uh, be with Jim, and may we search him out and find him. Please return your black-hearted, matted woolen sheep soul to us soon. Amen."

Chris raised an eyebrow and looked at Shep, slightly blushing from the intimate moment, and nervously laughed, saying, "Amen."

CHAPTER 12

Gentlemen, Start Your Engines

Shep looked at the lineup of cars with satisfaction. His Ford truck, the rabbi's Dodge Challenger, and Hector's El Camino. He clapped his hands, looked up at the blue June sky, and said, "What a great day for a race!"

"Rev it up, Rabbi!"

Rabbi David put his foot on the pedal. *Vroom*, the engine responded. Rabbi had arrived in his 1970 Dodge Challenger hot rod at Shep's request. The hot pink—technically Pink Panther color—with black stripes and shaker hood was an eye-catcher.

"Looking forward to seeing what that Challenger's got today, Rabbi."

Rabbi David often filled in as chaplain if Shep needed him, visiting with patients in the hospital. Rabbi and Shep might have differed on theology but not on serving the patients. Besides, it was all ecumenical.

"She will show you." He pushed the accelerator again to make the engine rev and the shaker hood rattle. The rabbi didn't look like a racecar driver in his black-brimmed hat, clean-shaven beard, and glasses. His slight frame made it look like he needed a booster seat to rise above the steering wheel.

Hector revved it up in his souped-up green El Camino with wood-grain paneling on the sides to show what it could do.

Rabbi David and Hector were cooing their racing engines at the parking lot turned drag strip when a slight putt-putt sound approached from behind.

Bob, from maintenance, waved as he drove the golf cart to their side and said, "Just made it in time!" Red, white, and blue crepe paper streamers flowed around the sides of the golf cart.

"Ha! Way to go!" Shep chuckled with everyone else at the absurdity that the golf cart would have any chance in this race.

Patients with walking privileges had begun to gather, Olivia among them.

"Good afternoon, Olivia. Good to see you outside here. Would you like to drop the flag for us today?" Shep held a black-and-white checked racing flag in his hand.

"I guess I could. What do I have to do?"

"Give everyone a moment to line up, and when I give you the signal"—he moved his hand up and down—"just drop the flag from high to low."

"Sure, okay. My boyfriend, Allen, is here visiting me today. I'm sure he'll gladly help me. He loves cars." She pointed him out to Shep across the parking lot.

"Oh good!" Shep waved to him. "Once you and Allen see everyone is ready, he can yell, 'Gentlemen, start your engines.'"

"Okay." She took the flag from Shep.

The paved parking lot behind the chapel served as the racetrack. Shep had drawn a line with chalk for the race lineup. The drivers pulled their cars and carts to the starting line and readied themselves. Allen and Olivia walked to the left side to be next to the lineup. Allen lovingly looked at Olivia to make sure she was ready.

The afternoon was fresh and warm, as spring had turned to summer at Hopewell Hill. The drivers strapped themselves to their seats—hands fervently on the steering wheels, ready for the high-speed chase. They revved their engines.

A peacock strutted in front of the drivers as if to say, "This is my area, and you should have asked permission for today's race." Allen shooed him across the lot to some side bushes and returned to his position next to Olivia.

"Gentlemen, start your engines!" Allen shrieked. The shaker throttled, the Ford whistled, the El Camino hummed, and Bob blew the golf cart horn.

A moment later, Shep gave Olivia the hand signal. She waved the black-and-white checkered flag back and forth.

They pushed off, and Rabbi's wheels screeched, leaving skid marks on the pavement. Shep pushed the pedal to the floor but didn't gain much speed in the '50s Ford, and the golf cart moved forward with a rattle. Hector's El Camino sounded mean and kept pace with the rabbi. The two were clearly in the lead.

"Whoo-hoo!" some patients on the sidelines screamed in unison as the golf cart passed them. They were waving their hands and laughing. Riker was barking, jumping, and twirling on the sidelines with them. Expressionless ashen faces changed to smiles and laughter as they watched the comical race unfold.

Sharon stood at Chris's open office door and knocked on it gently

Chris was on the phone but waved her in.

"Okay, I'll check with accounting on that." She hung up the phone. "What can I do for you, Sharon? I am so glad to see you. Not often do you make it over to my building."

"I know. I just finished my overnight and hung around to finish some paperwork, and I heard something I thought you might want to know."

"What?"

"Well, it's Shep."

"What about Shep?"

"There's a race going on."

"What? A race? What kind of race?" Chris put down her pen.

"A car race. It's on the chapel parking lot, but I thought you might want to know."

"A car race! What, when?"

"Now."

Chris rose from her desk. "Now!" She moved toward her door, and Sharon followed.

She hastily told Sharon goodbye and speed walked to the chapel. She seemed to float across the campus in her navy linen dress and taupe pumps. Anger fueled her walk.

She rounded the corner behind the chapel to the parking lot. Patients were on the grass laughing. One of them looked up and pointed at Chris, then they all scrambled, knowing Shep would probably be in trouble. Allen took Olivia by the elbow, and they gently walked through some trees and out of sight.

Chris walked to the other end of the parking lot. All the racecar drivers were out of their cars, cutting up about the winners and losers.

"Shep! What are you all doing?"

Shep looked up with sheer surprise. "Oh, hi, Chris! We are just having a little fun."

The maintenance boys jumped into the golf cart with Bob, Hector started up his El Camino, and they both whizzed away. Rabbi sat in his car, hollow and quiet as if hidden.

"Fun!" Chris moved closer to Shep, half whispering in his face so others could not see her venom. "We run a hospital, not a racetrack! You have taken staff away from their work and patients."

"What's the harm? Besides, we're on the chapel property, not the hospital's. Might I say you look lovely today, even if you're mad."

"Shep, don't try to use your looks and compliments to tamp down this crazy situation. Do you think this is what you should do with your time, my staff, and our patients?" She felt a strange flutter in her stomach as he smiled at her.

"Compliments? I should hold races more often. It's fun to see you get this excited." Shep wiped his brow with a mischievous look. "Besides that, I think we found him."

"What? What are you talking about now?"

"I have a lead on Jim. Jason from the Rib Shack thinks he's down in Atlantic City and gave me a lead on his whereabouts. I'm going down there to find him. Rabbi is here to fill in for me for a few days."

"Atlantic City. Of course, it would be AC." Chris slapped her hand on her leg. "I'm going with you."

"Chris, I think it's best to let me see if I can find him. Talk some sense into him. The rabbi will take care of the chapel and patient rounds."

He motioned over to Rabbi David. The rabbi smiled while exiting his car and doffed his hat to Chris out of respect.

Chris nodded back reluctantly.

"Okay, Shep, okay. At least he could still be in New Jersey. Just let me know where and when you find him. And no more of this race nonsense! We could get a serious write-up from the state about this." She shook her head and started walking away.

Just then a black BMW pulled into the adjacent parking lot, and a man in a blue suit stepped out.

"Chris!" he waved.

"Oh. Hi Spencer, what are you doing here?" She walked toward him.

Chris turned back to Shep. "Good luck finding Jim in Atlantic City. You're going to need it."

Shep nodded and watched Chris walk over to greet Spencer. He kissed Chris on the cheek. Something just didn't seem right to Shep about the pair, but for the life of him, he didn't know why.

CHAPTER 13

Under the Stars

The Brigantine Beach was calm. Shep lay in the bed of his truck on a makeshift mattress of several blankets, looking up at the stars. Like diamonds, they shone brightly. The moon illuminated the curling foam-topped waves of the Atlantic Ocean. Each wave sang a new verse of an ocean song.

Shep sighed and said, "Isn't this wonderful, Rike? Lullabied by the music of the waves is a perfect way to go to sleep."

Riker seemed well contented in the bed of the truck next to Shep. His sheepdog eyes batted lovingly at his master.

"This will be perfect tonight. Nothing like fresh Atlantic Sea air to make for a good night's sleep, and the room rate is cheap, but oh, the view. Hopefully, we'll be out of sight of the beach patrol, where we backed in and parked behind this berm. They allow four-wheel-drive cars on this beach. Don't you think our antique truck with four wheels counts, Riker?

"We'll make our way to Atlantic City in the morning. Bet those people over there"—he pointed to the casino lights across the inlet—"don't know how lovely it is on this island, or they would be with us in the back of this pickup enjoying the fresh smell of the Atlantic and our light show overhead! Well, good night, Rike."

Shep thought about tomorrow's mission as he closed his eyes while patting Riker. "The word from Jason is that Jim won big at one of the card tables when he first arrived, so big that he's been staying in a fancy hotel suite. But his luck turned quickly, and now he's getting kicked out." Shep began to doze off.

Morning came. The taste of salt was in Shep's mouth. He stood up in the back of the truck and stretched, arms wide. "Riker, we should do this more often. Nothing like sleeping under a heavenly blanket. Wasn't that refreshing!"

He rolled his pant legs up, and Riker came along as they walked along the beach. "Lord, please help me find Jim. Chris is counting on me." They walked along the shoreline and enjoyed the cool ocean water at their feet and paws.

"Come on now, Riker, let's go. Let's stop in at the Pirates Den for some breakfast. I've heard they have great banana pancakes; plus, Jason let me know some of the casino musclemen like to hang out there. Maybe we'll get a breakfast sandwich for you. I think we should try it while we're here, aye, aye, mate?"

Riker barked and ran to the truck.

Shep shut the tailgate and carefully drove off the beach to avoid making ruts in the sand and getting stuck.

As he drove, Shep sang along with the radio to the Drifters' song "Under the Boardwalk." His fingers tapped the steering wheel as he sang along. When they arrived, the popular local restaurant was bustling. The breakfast crowd carried out morning coffees. Riker whined to come in but sat in the truck, waiting for treats.

Shep entered the little house, which looked nothing like a pirate's den. The place resembled a beach cottage, and the ocean waves were not far away. The hostess seated Shep next to three men with big muscles, tight T-shirts, and tattoos. They spoke in deep, throaty voices.

"The special today is banana pancakes with peach mango maple syrup," the waitress said as she set a water glass in front of Shep and filled it.

"Wow, that sounds delicious! Can I have the pancakes, a hot tea, and a seawall breakfast sandwich with bacon for my mate outside in the truck?" Shep nodded to the window, where Riker leaned, panting, over the truck bed.

She turned to look. "Oh, cute. What kind is he?"

"A Border collie. He's a great friend."

"I'm sure he is." The waitress smiled as she took the menu. "I have a little terrier at home. We love our doggies, don't we?" She chewed her gum and winked.

Shep smiled and nodded as he sipped his water. The men beside Shep kept their conversation low, but Shep listened intently.

"Yeah, he's hanging up to dry, you might say. Ha, ha."

They all snickered.

"The look on his face when we left him hanging at the top of that old Ferris wheel! Wonder if he's still breathing."

"Yeah, Larry, you roughed him up pretty good. He could have had a heart attack."

"Yeah, well, the Lone Ranger deserved a few punches. He needs to understand who's boss around here. Maybe he hung there last night and thought about how he could come up with our dough."

"Let's see if Jim's poker cards can save him now. What a Ferris wheel cowboy. When we get to AC this morning, we'll see if he has figured out how to come up with the money."

They snickered and flexed their tanned muscles. Shep could see a dog bone imprinted on the right fleshy bicep of the nearest man. Flexing made the dog bone look like a bone you would feed a St. Bernard. It was so big. The inscription said, "Me Bad."

Shep's mind raced. *Jim! Ferris wheel in Atlantic City? I thought that indoor amusement park had closed. I know that place. It sounds like they have my Jim. They've left him for dead!*

Shep quickly ate a few bites of pancakes after they were delivered and plotted his next move. He put the seawall biscuit in a napkin, swallowed a last sip of tea, got up, and nodded to the waitress and the gang of pirates. Shep put a twenty on the table and walked to the truck.

"Here, Riker, get up into the front seat. Pretend this is a drive-thru. You can eat this up here. We're in a hurry!" Shep handed him the biscuit, and Riker gulped it quicker than a sea monster might swallow a whale, licking his mouth afterward.

They drove fifteen minutes across the causeway to Atlantic City across from the beach.

Shep entered the casino—he knew the one—and the sound of slot machines ringing with bells and whistles besieged his senses. Card tables were tucked into a corner where men and women in black-and-white uniforms were dealing cards. The stale cigarette air was pungent. Compared with the fresh sea breeze right outside the door, Shep couldn't understand why anyone would choose this over that.

An area once an entryway to the entertainment complex had a sign that said CLOSED FOR CASINO ENHANCEMENT—COMING SOON. Shep looked for a way behind these doors. He was sure this was where the Ferris wheel was, and hopefully his friend Jim Warren. Observing from a distance, Shep noticed a swinging door where the staff went in and out, adjusting their uniforms. He moved in closer, and after the card dealers seemed to start their shift and the doorway grew quiet, Shep slipped through the door.

He passed undetected through the dressing room corridor. Seeing yet another door, he went through this and began walking through the old entertainment complex filled with bumper cars, pinball machines, shops, and snack bars, all shuttered. It was dark inside, as the management had ensured no one would see this failed complex anymore. Boardwalk-style chairs on wheels that took patrons through tunnels recalling Atlantic City's history lay dormant. As Shep stood in the center of the indoor theme park, the hundred-foot Ferris wheel towered over him. With windows at the top of the complex, the Ferris wheel ride offered an ocean view from inside. Shep moved in closer and stood directly under the Ferris wheel. The orange, red, yellow, and blue cars stood still.

"Jim, you up there?"

Nothing. No answer. Going closer until he was just under one of the red seats, he looked up again and saw a pair of cowboy boots hanging from a blue cart. The boots hung motionless. "Jim! Jim!"

Shep's heart sank. The musclemen did hang him up there! His heart began to beat faster, adrenaline kicking in. As his mind raced, he thought, *How will I get him out of here if he is still alive? The pirate gang is undoubtedly on its way.*

Shep moved inside the wheel's huge steel circle and began climbing. He worked his way up. He grabbed each piece of steel as he worked his body toward the top. Only the sound of metal and swinging carts could be heard.

"Dead or alive, I have to reach you, Jim Warren." Every time he catapulted past another colored carriage, it would swing. Then, upward again, he neared the blue one where Jim was dangling. Looking down occasionally, Shep was thankful no one, either staff or Bad to the Bone, was on his trail yet.

Finally, he came to the carriage where Jim was hanging. Shep hurled and hoisted himself onto the floorboard of the carriage and then leaned in toward Jim. Hanging by a rope wrapped underneath his arms onto the front carriage bar, Jim looked rough. His right eye was blackened, and he had several cuts on the left side of his face, but he was breathing.

"Jim, Jim, are you okay?" Jim's head slumped over to one side. "Jim! Jim! Wake up!" Shep touched his face as the rest of his body hung below the car. "What did they do to you? Come on, buddy, wake up!" Jim squinted through his left eye.

"Shep? Shep," he muttered. "What, what you doin' here?"

"I came here to find you. What kind of trouble did you get yourself into, Jim?"

"I ... I ..."

"Listen, it doesn't matter now. We've just got to get you out of here. Listen, Jim, and listen good! Jim!" Shep nudged Jim's face and looked at him with empathy but urgency. "Stay with me. Wake up. Are you with me? Listen to what I tell you!"

Jim nodded. "Okay, okay."

"Here is what we are going to do. I am going to untie this rope from the carriage."

"NO!" Jim yelled.

"You won't fall, trust me. You must trust me, Jim. I will lower you down slowly, very slowly. Listen, we don't have much time. Me Bad and friends are on your trail. You have to do as I am telling you."

"Me Bad?" Jim got a terrified look in his eyes. "How do you know them?"

"Don't worry about that now. Let's just get you down from here."

Jim nodded.

Shep untied the knots holding Jim to the carriage, bracing himself inside the carriage. He slowly let the rope down a little at a time.

"Easy. Easy, Preacher!"

"Just don't look down, Jim."

The carriage swung back and forth at each jerk in the rope as Shep continued to lower Jim. About midway down, the poker cards in Jim's T-shirt pocket came loose and tumbled like confetti all around him through the air—aces, ten of diamonds, six of spades, and the whole fifty-two-card deck swirled beneath the cowboy like a flock of seagulls.

CHAPTER 14

Wildflower

"Jim, Jim, are you okay?" Shep rushed to Jim's side.

"I'm okay, but that was a good deck of cards."

Jim wiped his brow with a shaky wrist as he struggled to stand up, staggering. Rope burns were on his wrists and chest after being bound at the top of the Ferris wheel for a night.

"Glad you made it down safe, cowboy. Now let's get you out of here. Let's go this way. The Me Bads will be back for you soon." Shep put Jim's arm around his shoulder to give him support. Jim held on tightly, sweat pouring down his battered face.

Through the corridor and into the casino, a few gamblers looked up from their noisy slot machines and stared at the pair. Seeing a security guard in the near distance, Shep immediately turned in the other direction to the opposite exit. As they did, Shep looked back and saw the Me Bads enter the door they would have been exiting.

"Looks like we made it just in time, Jim. My truck is right over here."

"Ugh, yeah." Jim hobbled faster. "Let's get out of here."

Shep helped Jim into the truck, and his head immediately rested on the back of the seat from exhaustion.

Speeding away, Shep took the route to the Atlantic City Expressway. Windows down and the wind blowing on their faces, silence took over as the whitewalls of the green Ford turned one mile after another and away from danger.

Jim dozed off, and Shep kept driving toward home, toward Hopewell.

Shep thought about everything Jim must have been through these last weeks in Atlantic City. Now to culminate it in an almost-death experience was all Jim needed and, for that matter, Chris. He wished Jim could stop his gambling ways and reconcile with Chris. It seemed so simple but so hard at the same time. He looked over at Jim. His white beard was clammy with sweat. Wrinkles and lines on his face added to the weariness of this whole situation. To Shep, it seemed like each line on Jim's face was a road map of loneliness, traveling in all directions. The only destination at the end of each wrinkle was suffering. Gambling had Jim encircled, and it seemed there was no way out.

Shep's mobile phone rang. Hopewell Hill was the incoming number.

"Hey there."

"Shep, it's me. It's Chris. What is happening down in AC? How is it going?"

"I have Jim. He's in the truck with me now. We're on our way back."

"Oh, great! Wow, was it tough finding him?"

"Well, it wasn't too bad. Let's just say it had its highs and its lows."

"Highs and lows? I'm not sure I want to know."

"It was a little crazy, but I can catch you up on that later. Do you want me to take Jim to the hotel for now?"

"Sure, that'll work. I'll call the hotel and make the arrangements. Thank you, Shep. Thanks for all you have done. Really. By the way, Rabbi David has been doing a great job with the patients while you've been gone."

"I am glad to hear that."

"One more thing, though. The Hill isn't the same without you. Maybe a bit calmer, but not the same."

Shep smiled. "Is that right? Well, I'll be back soon to stir things up. No worries. See you soon." He hung up, and a warm feeling moved through him. He cleared his throat and did a little drumbeat on the steering wheel. He repositioned himself in his seat and turned to check on Riker. Riker looked at Shep through the back window. He barked at the wind as it swept through his fur like a fan at high speed.

Shep looked at Jim sleeping and then out the window to the adjacent fields. He felt the noonday summer sun with his hand in the wind. Jim seemed much like the yellow and lilac wildflowers on the side of the highway, growing untamed and wild. God was the only one who could nurture any possible blossom in Jim's heart before it was too late. Too late, and the blooms and Jim's heart would wither in the August heat.

Jim startled awake as Shep slowed and pulled into the Crown Hotel. "Where are we?" Recognizing the run-down hotel, Jim balked. "Oh, no. Not here. I want to go home!"

"We are home," Shep said. "Back in Hopewell. Let's get you settled in, and you can take a shower." Shep helped Jim from the truck and up to his room.

Shep got them something to eat from the corner takeout and ensured that Jim was secure and comfortable. He closed the door and told Jim he would return in the morning.

The following day Chris arrived at the Crown Hotel to check on Jim. She wore jeans and a crisp white shirt. At first, she knocked softly on Jim's hotel door. There wasn't an answer. She knocked again. Silence. Hitting harder, she raised her voice. "Jim. Jim, are you in there? It's Chris. I'm here, here to check on you." She knocked again. "Are you in there?"

"Go away. You don't need to mess with me. You're finished with me."

"Jim, open up. I want to talk to you."

She could hear some noise that sounded like Jim might have tripped over some furniture. She pulled her hair back and put her ear against the door. "Jim, come on! Open up!"

"I'm coming. I'm coming. Give a guy a minute."

As Jim fiddled with the knob, Chris took a deep breath. He opened the door as far as the chain lock would allow it.

"What do you want?" Jim's swollen, blackened eye looked through the opening at Chris.

"Oh! Oh boy. What happened to you?"

"Just a little roughed up, that's all."

"Jim, I want to talk to you. You're back, and we have some things to work out."

"We've got nothin' to talk about. I lost. Those casinos are rigged against the cardholders."

"Let me in. Let's talk about it."

Jim yanked the chain off the holder. "Come in, but I've got nothing to say. Except I am going home."

Chris pushed the door open, and Jim returned to his hotel bed. He was wearing jeans and a wrinkled shirt, halfway buttoned.

"Jim, why did you run away? Why did you leave here?"

"I didn't run away. I went to Atlantic City to make some money. It's what I do."

"What you do? What you need to do is get yourself together. We need some time to work on your problem, Jim."

"I don't have a problem. You medical types think you can fix anything, don't you? Even if it doesn't need fixing!" Jim's face was now red with anger.

"Look, what do you want, Jim?"

"Are you married, Chris?"

"Why are you switching the subject? And no, I am not married."

"Just wondered why you would be spending time on me. It seems like you might have a husband by now."

"By now! By now! Let me tell you what I have been doing by now. If you don't mind! I have been working my butt off to make something of myself. With no help from you, I might add! You do have the gall to ask stuff like that."

"Listen, Chris. I didn't mean it that way. I just thought …"

"You thought you would get the subject from you and onto me. Well, you are mistaken. I am not the one who needs fixing here."

"Oh, that's what it is. I'm your little project. You want to fix me so you can come back here and tell Helen that you turned Jim around, turned a sinner into a saint. How nice."

"Mom doesn't have anything to do with this. Except if it weren't for her, I would be nowhere!"

"Okay, you said it, Chris. Your loser dad helped you with nothin'. That is exactly my point, my point in leaving. You don't want me around here. You have your life, and it doesn't include me."

Just then, there was a knock at the door.

"Who are you expecting? Jim?"

"No one."

"It's me, Shep. Open up, Jim."

Chris looked at Jim and sighed. She went to the door and opened it, her wooden beaded bracelets rattling when she turned the doorknob. She looked at Shep with her blue-green eyes. "What are you doing here?"

"Chris. Chris, I didn't know you would be here." Shep was juggling two coffees in a to-go holder. Caught off guard, he almost dropped the carrier.

"Well, come on in and join the get-Jim-in-line party," Jim announced.

Blushing a bit, Shep asked, "May I come in, Chris?"

"Sure. Just sure."

"Can I get you a coffee, Chris?"

"No, I'm fine."

Shep came in and sat down in one of the side chairs.

"How are you feeling this morning, Jim? How is that eye? Could you use some ice?"

"No, I don't want ice."

"Look, Jim, I know how much you've been talking about home. You muttered it the whole way back from Atlantic City." Shep looked at Chris, tapping her arm. "Tell us about your home."

Jim took the coffee from Shep and sipped it. "Home, for me, is different depending on my mood. I can be home at the casinos, at the card table, and I can be at home out in nature. I have ..."

"You have ... what, Jim?"

"Let's just say I have my place. I like to go. And the mountains are part of that. They make a man out of you. I feel at home there."

Chris became quiet and still. "Okay. Mountains. Nature. What's not to love? What if I go with you to those mountains? It's been a long time since I've been back in Idaho. I can get you home and gather your things, and we can come back here."

"Come back here? I don't know about that." Jim shuffled in his bed.

"That would be the condition. Go out there, see around, return here."

Shep looked at Jim earnestly. "Jim, would you like that? Would you like to go home?"

"I sure would. I sure would."

"Perfect. I'll book some flights for us tomorrow."

"Chris, I didn't know you were a wild-west type, and what about your work?" Shep said.

She turned and looked at Shep. "I have some time off coming, and actually, I would like to see Jim's mountains."

"Well, I have another idea. We could have Cal fly us out in his taildragger. It's perfect for navigating the mountain terrain. We could be on our own schedule."

"Not a bad idea, but who said anything about us?" Chris made a triangle with her fingers. Meaning, Jim, Shep, and herself. "And Shep, don't you have work?"

"Rabbi David is doing a pretty good job. I might as well let him continue a little longer. Besides, Cal likes me to help him navigate."

"Well, giddy-up. Let's go." Jim's bruised face looked at peace.

CHAPTER 15

Home

Shep closed the white picket gate behind him as he walked up the sidewalk to the front door of his A-frame house in Ewing. Imprints of Annie were everywhere, beginning with the flower gardens. Peonies and roses dotted the front beds. Sometimes coming home for Shep was comforting, and other days without Annie there, it seemed like a gray cloud enveloped the whole place. He flung his duffel bag on one of the leather chairs, which Annie used to sink into with an oversized cream sweater on and a cup of coffee in her hand. Her brunette hair would softly fall around her face as she smiled at Shep. More memories filled the bookshelves. Framed pictures of hikes they took together and Christmas season photos of the two picking out the perfect tree. All before the incident with her father landed Shep in prison, and later Annie was going through cancer. The memories were bittersweet, but it was home. Shep couldn't imagine what home meant for Jim. Where was home for a gambler like Jim? Where was he thinking about when he muttered, "I want to go home?"

"Cal, it's me, Shep." Shep paced over the wide-planked pine floors in his home as he spoke on the phone.

"How are you?"

"Well, pretty good. I hope all is well with your family."

"Yes, we're doing fine, and you?"

"Good. Good. But I have a little problem, Cal. I need … well, I need to get to the Sawtooths."

"The Sawtooths? I thought you were chasing your boss's cowboy father in Atlantic City."

"Well, technically, she's not my boss. I have my jurisdiction with the chapel. And, yes, I was looking for Jim."

"Did you find him?"

"Yes, and, well, I, I freed him like a bird, so to speak."

"Why do you bother with him, Shep?"

"He needs help. He just doesn't know how much, and Chris could use help with him too. He can be a lot to handle alone."

"I'm beginning to think you have a thing for helping this guy and, maybe most of all, a thing for his daughter," Cal joked.

"Where did you come up with that idea?" Shep's face felt hot. A tingle went down his neck, and he nervously ran his hand through his dark hair.

"I don't know. It's just something about the sound of your voice when you say her name."

"I think you're working too much and need a flying break. It's just business. If we fly Jim out to gather his belongings and get him back here to where Chris can begin dealing with him, it will help her greatly."

"You're willing to do that for her?"

"Look, she has helped me a lot in the past. Getting to Hopewell Hill after prison and when Annie got sick, she rallied the hospital around us. If I can help her now, I would gladly do it."

"Hmm, I get that part, I guess. But how do you know the Sawtooth Mountains are his home? Does he live in a cave in the woods out there? Come on. Besides, you have about a month and a half before winter begins in the mountains."

"That's why we should take him out there as soon as possible. Jim will show us where his home is. Aren't you up for a little cross-country trip?"

"Shep, you know how tempting it is for me to fly anytime, but I don't know. That's a long trip. A trip like that takes some planning. I would have to move my patients' scheduling all around. Let me get back to you and let you know. Are you sure you want to help someone who is so difficult to deal with and claims he has a home where we don't know the actual location? Does that sound logical to you, Shep?"

"It sounds very logical. Phone me later after you've thought about it. The four of us and Riker will have a great time!"

"Hold on, Shep. I don't know about this. Who said anything about your dog?"

"Riker? He's a great travel mate. Talk to you soon."

Shep hung up the phone quickly. He pumped his fist in the air as a sign of victory. He knew Cal could not turn down an opportunity, a reason to fly to Idaho. Riker began whirling around the house, sensing Shep's excitement. Shep assured him he was going with him, so soon, Riker tired out and took a nap next to the front door.

Shep looked over at Riker. "Wish Jim would stick as close to me as you, Riker. We'd have a lot less trouble."

Another call was a must—the rabbi. Shep thought he had better check in with him.

The hospital operator answered. "Hopewell Hill, how can I help you?"

Shep said, "Grace Chapel, please."

"Is that you, Shep?"

"Yes, it is! How are you, Marjorie?"

"I'm good, Shep."

"How are things going around there? Give me the scoop!"

"Pretty good."

"Are you getting to know the rabbi?"

"Well, yes," she said with hesitation.

"What does that mean?"

"Everything is okay, and the rabbi is a doll, but we miss you on the softball team. We got beat by the occupational group last Wednesday night. We need you, so come back soon," Marjorie said as she chewed her gum loudly.

"Oh, too bad you guys couldn't beat them. I always like to shake those guys up."

"I'll connect you to the chapel, Shep."

The phone rang. "Rabbi David here."

"Hi, Rabbi. It's Shep."

"Well now, Shep, I know a fella by that name."

"Aw now, Rabbi! How is it going? Seeing lots of patients?"

"Yes. Every time I help you out here, Shep, I realize what a big job you have. So many needy people."

"Yes, it is true every day at Hopewell Hill. Keep up the good work, Rabbi. I'm not sure when I'll return; I have a little errand to run. Well, maybe a big errand. Can you take care of the place for a while longer?"

"Yes, sure I can. You know I'm retired; don't mind it a bit. It gives me something to do. Did you find that cowboy you were looking for?"

"Yes, yes, I did. It was a wild ride, but Jim is back here now."

CHAPTER 16

Yurts

Chris's mobile phone was ringing.

"That's me. I'll just take that over here a second." Chris walked over to the corner of the hangar and spoke in a low voice. "Hi, Spence. Yes, I called yesterday. Just wanted to let you know I'll be out of town for a bit. I'll be in Idaho. Yes, I know it's a little unusual, but I have some responsibilities to tend to with my father, you know. What? Oh, the hospital chaplain and his friend, the pilot, are along on the trip. Ha, yes, no worries over the chaplain. For sure. Well, I'll call you when I return. Okay, thanks, Spence. See you soon."

"I'm ready. Ready." Chris cleared her throat and looked at Shep, who was standing nearby. "Just had to take that call minute."

"Sure, understand." Shep nodded.

"We're ready to fly." Cal made his final checks on the Cessna 180.

"I don't know how or why I let a fool-headed preacher talk me into such illogical things as this, but let's go," Cal said.

The Cessna 180 was ready and fueled. The trip to Idaho would require four overnight stops for fueling and maintenance. Cal loaded the back of the Skywagon with duffel bags and hiking provisions while Shep hopped in the front seat, and Chris and Jim sat in the back. Riker sat in the middle.

Shep looked back at Jim and Chris as Cal checked his instruments. "This is going to be an adventure!"

Chris and Jim smiled at Shep and nodded, and Chris patted Riker as he panted. Cal looked back and motioned for everyone to have their headgear on to communicate in flight. He gave a thumbs-up, and they all responded the same way. He then began taxiing down the runway after getting the all-clear from the control tower.

In a few minutes, they were gaining speed. Slowly, as Cal pulled back on the throttle, the Cessna rose up and into the air. Chris looked at Jim, and he at her. They smiled.

They were on their way, on their way to Jim's "home" in Idaho. For now, as they looked down on the expansive land squares and the late September golden sun cresting the wings of the Cessna, there was a sense of peace.

"Can you imagine the creator of all this?" Shep spanned his hands toward the windows as he spoke into his microphone headpiece. "It is just spectacular."

Cal smiled, showing his pure joy in flying, getting up and above the ground noise of life.

"Well, I'll say he had a big job," Jim said.

Chris just smiled.

The trip was long, and Chris had brought reports from work and read data from the hospital to pass the hours. Jim slept while Riker rested his black-and-white head on his lap.

The overnight stops at Toledo, De Moines, and Fort Collins were welcomed by everyone. A chance to get a hot meal and rest.

Finally, the Smiley Creek airstrip was in sight in a beautiful valley surrounded by jagged mountains at the base of the Sawtooth National Forest. The mowed summer grass strip stood out from the air, ready for landing. Cal moved the yoke and flipped the controls in and out as he guided the plane in the mountain breeze. With skill, he aced it and glided into a smooth landing. The Cessna Skywagon touched down on the grass strip, with only a few bumps on the grassy terrain. The plane came to a slowdown, and the propeller whirled to a stop. Cal flipped more switches ensuring the engine wheezed down. Shep took off his headphones and gave Cal a fist bump. "Way to go, my friend!" Riker stood as best he could in the back seat and barked.

Cal said, "Well, we are not in Jersey anymore."

"That's for sure!" said Shep.

They unlatched their seat belts and stepped out of the plane. The cool breeze hit their faces as everyone climbed out. Shep stood with arms open wide and took in the clear air. "Nothing like fresh mountain air." Riker bounced from the plane, circled it, and ran down the airstrip and back like a freed prisoner.

The caretaker came out to greet them. "Welcome to Smiley Creek! Glad to have you. My name is Tyler." He extended his hand.

Shep shook his rough hand with a firm grip. "Shep's my name."

Tyler wore a puffy blue ski vest, work boots, and faded jeans. A rugged-looking man in his thirties, he looked as if he might double as ski patrol on his off days. "What brings you out west? Hunting? Fishing?"

Jim said, "I brought my daughter out here with a couple of her friends to see my mountains."

"Well, great! Where are you headed today?" Tyler asked.

"I made arrangements for us to stay at the Galena Lodge tonight. Then tomorrow, we plan on heading into Ketchum," Cal explained.

"Okay, great. I'm going that way today—southeast, that is—and could give you a lift. It's on my way. My shift is about over."

"Very nice of you. That would be great if you have room for us and Shep's dog, Riker."

"Sure do. That's a good-looking dog you have there, Shep. I drive that blue Suburban over there." He pointed near the airport control base.

"Tyler, can I tie down my plane at one of your spaces on the side of the grass strip for a few days?"

"Absolutely. Take the first one you see. We have some beautiful planes parked here."

"Perfect, and yes, I noticed." Cal smiled.

They thanked Tyler for the lift, grabbed their backpacks and duffel bags, and headed toward his Suburban. The clouds moved across the peaks, causing shadows below. Little buttercup wildflowers blew in the wind at the edge of the grass strip. Much like these buttercups, they were like dots in this Idaho expanse.

The words Galena Lodge were etched into a log archway across the trail opening when they reached the main gate and entrance.

"Welcome to Galena Lodge," the front desk hiker-looking man announced.

"Oh, thank you. We have a reservation under Cal Richardson for four people. Two or three rooms," Chris said.

"Let me see. You have a reservation for two yurts." The reservationist looked up at Chris.

"Yurt? What's a yurt?" Chris's eyebrows raised. "We just need our hotel rooms."

"It's kind of like a tent," the reservationist said.

"A tent?" Chris cocked her head.

"Ma'am, I think you will find it quite comfortable. Our yurts can sleep up to six to eight people. They are furnished with wood stoves for the chilly nights here in Idaho, spring through fall. Well insulated, made of extreme wool from sheep from our region, and covered with weatherproof material. We have one small yurt reserved and a second accommodating three."

"This is the Taj Mahal compared with where I stay. Usually, when I'm traveling, it's just me, my mess kit, and a blanket," Jim said.

"Like I said, we aren't in Jersey anymore, Chris. The three guys can stay in one, and Chris, you can have the smaller one all to yourself." Cal mischievously smiled.

"I guess that'll work. This should be interesting." Chris slanted a smile.

The four of them and Riker followed the paths to their yurts. All the oatmeal-colored domed tents were situated at the mountain's base, snuggled near the forest line. As they all walked through the door to the larger yurt and looked up, they could see the inside design was an angled assembly of intricate beams in the rounded ceiling. An interior middle opening in the center crown, covered with glass, exposed the sky. Soft lighting illuminated the tent, and cot-like beds surrounded the room.

"This is a pretty good setup." Jim put his backpack on a cot. "I think I'll go outside and see what's around."

He stepped outside, where Cal was conversing about the lodge with one of the staff members.

Shep put his bags down. "Chris, let me help you with your bags to your yurt."

They walked on a trail over to the smaller yurt. Once inside, Shep put Chris's bags down and reached over to turn on a lantern by the bedside.

"Well, this is pretty cozy."

"It is nicer in here than I imagined," Chris said.

"Yes, and you must admit, this mountain air does something for the senses, doesn't it? Can't you already feel Hopewell Hill behind us, at least for a while?"

"Maybe so." Chris smoothed the dark-green linen coverlet on the pine bed. She stood on the red-and-blue oriental rug in her new hiking boots as she looked around the tent. A fireplace was across the room, and a welcome basket from guest services was on a table nearby.

"Let's start up this wood stove." He put a few logs from a basket of wood and struck a match to light the fire. In minutes, the smell was like an alpine dream.

"Shep, I just hope we can get out to Jim's place, wherever that is, get his things, and get back to Jersey as soon as possible."

"We will, but your father seems to be enjoying this for now. He already seems more relaxed."

"I'm not sure what more relaxed looks like with him. He has a lot of exterior layers, each one tougher than the next." Chris unpacked a few things and laid them on the bed.

"I'm sure that has built up over time, layers covering disappointments."

"Well, I've had a few myself, and look at me."

"Yes, look at you, in charge of a hospital and all."

Shep couldn't help but think of how the two were so different and similar—Jim hiding behind the truth that he was a washed-up aging gambler and Chris hiding behind the hurt of never having a father in her life, burying it in her career. Two layered onions.

"That's knocking off the chill. Nothing like a fire to help one relax." Shep rubbed his hands and warmed them next to the fire.

Chris neared the fire and did the same. "This is nice, and look at this." She turned to the table, where the welcome basket held wine and a few snacks, compliments of the house. "Would you like to open it and share a glass?"

"Sure, why not."

She sat down in the poufy club chair covered in flannel.

Shep opened the wine, poured two glasses, and handed one to Chris. "Cheers to you, Chris, for making this trip for your father." He held up his glass.

"Cheers to both of us and of course, Cal, can't forget him. Thank you, Shep, for taking this journey with me."

"I wouldn't want to be anywhere else."

They lifted their glasses with a clink and sipped the velvety wine.

Shep sat down across from Chris. The sun began setting outside, with nightfall soon behind, but they didn't seem to notice because the fire was crackling now.

Chris took off her boots, revealing a zigzag pattern in her woolen socks. "Do you miss her, Shep? Do you think of her every day?"

"Annie? Well, yes, I think of her often. She died so young. We were married for only seven years. I couldn't believe she got sick after I got out of prison. I just couldn't believe it."

"That must have been so hard. I know you thought you were going to have a fresh start. Especially after defending her in such a way. Saving her life from her own father. I initially read your story in the *Trenton Times* after Annie's father died. And I must say it intrigued me. Very valiant of you to defend Annie from her abusive father."

"Her dad, Joe, came to our house in a stupor that night. Drunk. He was outside on our porch. There was no way I was letting him get near Annie. I went outside to try to talk some sense into him. Words got heated. He lashed out and drew a gun. I tried to break it out of his hand, and the gun went off. Initially only wounded, he died later at the hospital."

"That is so tough."

"I don't question what I did, but if it had happened inside our home instead of outside the door, the laws and the jury could have found me not guilty since I was defending Annie, myself, and our home. I didn't want him getting in, getting close to her. He was evil."

Chris took another sip of wine.

"Anyway, doing some time, completing my chaplaincy program in prison, and thinking of getting home to Annie kept me going. And, of course, when I learned I would be getting an early release and applied for the job at Hopewell Hill, I can't tell you what that meant. What it meant to get the opportunity and what it does mean to work at such a place now with you."

"You had quite the story. Maybe it resonated with me because of Jim in some way. I felt for Annie and what you did for her. When we were looking for a chaplain and Lisa, our head of HR, was going through applicants, I saw your picture in the pile and remembered you." Chris cleared her throat a bit.

"I'm glad you did." Shep smiled.

"Well, I wish you had had more time with Annie once you got home."

"Me too. We had a lot of talks. She and I. This one time, near the end, the hospice nurse had been in and left our home. I was exhausted. I fell asleep in a chair next to her bed. When I awoke, she was lying there lovingly staring at me. She said in a still, soft voice, 'It's okay.' I said, 'Okay? What's okay?' Thinking it was something with her bed, her pain meds."

"It's okay to move on. After I'm gone." Shep's voice quivered. "She whispered to me, 'It's okay to find love again.'" A tear fell down his cheek.

"She was beautiful, Shep. The few times I met her at our annual fundraiser banquet, she seemed very sweet."

"She was. She was. What about you? Have you ever found that someone?"

Chris turned and gazed into the orange flames. "Once, in college, I was close to love, but he moved away for law school during my senior year. We planned that I would join him after graduation, but it never materialized. I guess it just wasn't meant to be. Then, of course, there is Spencer."

"Spencer, the guy in the BMW?"

"How do you know Spencer?" She raised her head and nodded. "Oh, yes, the day of your famous car races, he came to campus. Our families have known each other a long time. He has an insurance agency in town. I guess we casually date."

"Casually date, hmm. Okay."

"Well, then there is my work. It's a 24-7 job."

"That's a lot of hours. Doesn't leave much time for anything else."

They sat in silence while the fire crackled. Chris's eyes grew heavy, and she drifted off.

Shep got up and grabbed the plush beige throw on the end of her bed. He covered her, slipped out, and walked down the trail to his yurt.

CHAPTER 17

Old Gray

Morning came early, as Cal had asked everyone to rally by eight o'clock. "Get your coffee, and let's head over to the airport," he said.

Soon they were down the runway and up in the air for the short jump to Ketchum. The Galena Mountain range stood behind towering pines, and the aspen trees of autumn shimmered like lemon drops in the sun. In some folds of the mountain trails, from above, they could see herds of sheep moving, with ranchers on horseback. Collies were at the cowboys' lead on the sides of the sheep.

"They're trailing the sheep. This time of year brings back memories." Jim pointed to the mountain.

"What is that?" Chris asked.

"In the fall, ranchers move their flocks through these mountains, to the lower pastures and farms below, and then through the town of Ketchum. They've been doing it since the 1800s. In the last couple of years, the town of Ketchum has made a festival out of it. I worked these mountain ranges as a rancher several years back."

"That must have been fascinating," Shep said.

"It was. Those ranchers sure did count those sheep. We were responsible for always knowing where each of them was. We would run the herd down to greener pastures, let them graze, and then keep moving the next day. The ranchers and their dogs were always looking for any sheep that might get lost from the herd."

"That must have been hard work," Chris said.

"It was. I was a lot younger then, but it was great to be outdoors," Jim said. "One year, the ranch I was with had a sheep run loose from the pack, and he made his way up the mountain. The sheepdogs tried to work him back, but we lost him. We nicknamed him Old Gray because we knew that lost and alone in the craigs of those mountain tops"—Jim pointed across to the vast Galena Range—"he would turn gray and matted. Soon, he would be weighed down with fleece because of not being sheared in so long. So every one of us kept looking for Old Gray every year as we ran those sheep down the valley. It kind of became something of a legend, the legend of Old Gray.

"Did you ever find Old Gray?" Shep asked.

"Well, one late afternoon we stopped and settled the herd for the day. One of the sheepdogs came barking into camp." Jim looked over at Riker and patted him on the head. "This dog, Winnie, was going crazy, whirling around and around until we got up to see what she was trying to tell us."

"Sometimes Riker does the same thing."

"Charlie and me, the rancher I was working with, saddled up our horses and followed Winnie up the mountain. It was starting to get dark. She led us into some tight caverns up there. Finally, we got to a bit of a cave entrance, and Winnie stopped and sat right in front of it. It was dusk now. I got off my horse and took a few steps into the opening. Deep in the cave, I could see a set of beady eyes staring out. All I could see were those eyes. Heck, if it had been Halloween, I might have started running." Jim chuckled.

"Sometimes, we get ourselves into a mess just like Old Gray. We think we can do everything ourselves, but we need a shepherd," Shep said softly.

"Yeah, I guess in some ways, I'm no different than Old Gray." Jim's eyes grew serious.

Silence. "What did you do then, Jim?" Chris asked.

"Well ..." Jim sighed. "That Old Gray was in an old gray mess! He was unable to help himself. His matted wool hadn't been sheared for several years, making him unable to move. We had to sleep at the cave entrance that night and bring him down in the sunlight the next day."

"Kind of reminds me of when you had to deliver that breached foal," Chris said.

With astonishment, Jim said, "I didn't know you remembered that."

"How did you get Old Gray down?" Cal asked.

"We went into the cave in the morning and pulled Old Gray out. He wasn't happy about it, I tell you. This guy was miserable and helpless under the weight of his fleece. We tied his front feet to a long branch from a tree. Old Gray's front feet to one end and the back feet to the other. Then we carried him down the mountain, upside down, the branch between the two horses. Old Gray was baaing loudly. But it had to be done. We had to get him back to camp, to the bottom of the mountain, and shear all the matted, foul wool from him so he would have a chance to make it. He returned to his feet again, ate, and joined the rest of the herd after a while. The other ranchers couldn't believe Winnie had led us to him. She was a real dog hero." Jim rubbed one of Riker's ears.

"That is some story, Dad." Chris cleared her throat.

Cal continued to fly the Cessna low enough to get a view of all the action of the sheep moving down the mountain. The sheep kicked up dust as they ran along the mountain trails, sheepdogs on their edges, keeping them on the path, and cowboys on their horses driving them forward.

Riker began to whine and jumped into Jim's lap.

Jim stroked him. "Oh, now, if you don't be careful, I'll put you in the Sheep Dog Trials and test to see how you would fare at moving those sheep."

Everyone chuckled.

They landed and went from Ketchum airport via a taxi into town. Rustic saloon-type-looking buildings lined the main street in Ketchum. Jim told the taxi driver, "Drop us off at Whiskey Jacks. We'll go see Leslie, a friend of mine. She runs the place."

The four entered Whiskey Jacks. The bar made a U shape, and patrons were already soaking themselves with drinks and stroking their beards. Gem-colored bottles displayed their liquid along the wall. Saloon shutter doors were swinging on the other side of the room, revealing card tables. As the waitress came back and forth through the doors, poker players could be seen eyeing their cards. Across the room, the only window displayed the beautiful mountain range, and sunlight broke through the smokey atmosphere.

A woman approached. "Jim, where ya been?" She had frizzy blond hair and a cigarette voice. Her skin looked as dry as the land they were in.

"Leslie! Come over here."

"I wasn't sure when we would see you again. Who do you have here with you?"

"This is my daughter, Chris, and some of her friends."

"Daughter! I didn't know you had kids. Guess someone tamed you at some time."

Jim laughed hauntingly.

"Nice to meet you, Leslie. These are my friends, Shep and Cal," Chris said.

"I heard you went back East, Jim. I wasn't sure if we'd see ya again around here. Now, you gotta promise to not go so crazy at that poker table." She nodded in that direction.

Outside, the excitement was building for the run of the sheep through the town, which was happening soon. Children could be heard yelling, "Here they come!"

"We better get out there to see this," Shep said.

"They really make their way through the town itself?" Chris asked.

"Yes, they come off the mountain, like I said before, and go through the town to the pastures below," Jim said.

Chris, Shep, Cal, and Jim made their way through the crowd to an open spot for viewing.

As the baa of sheep drew closer, the children jumped up and down with glee.

Dots of white and black sheep with dogs guiding them and cowboys on horseback descended upon the town. White, furry coats and hooves padded the streets. Hundreds, if not thousands, of sheep came through. The crowd was told to be a little still and quiet, so as not to scare the sheep too much.

Suddenly, Riker, nervously pacing on the sidelines, bolted into the crowd of sheep.

"Riker!" Shep ran after him.

Jim ran into the crowd to help, and soon, Cal and Chris were in the mix following the sheep parade. Riker ran fast ahead, and everyone was lost within the herd of sheep.

With sheep baaing here and there, Chris stumbled along with them as they stepped on her boots.

Shep pushed through the crowd to get closer to Chris. "Are you okay?"

"Yes, just having to go with it." Chris laughed and suddenly was twirled around by a sheep moving across the herd.

"Well, Riker's instincts got the best of him!" Shep yelled.

Finally, they were able to get off to the side of the herd, and they fell on a bench laughing. As it quieted, Riker came panting and wagging his tail toward Shep, and Cal found them all on the sidelines.

"That was quite a thrill. I didn't know we were going to be part of the sheep parade!" Cal said.

Chris looked up and down the street as the parade finished. "Oh my gosh, that was crazy. Wait—where's Jim?"

All three looked at one another and scanned the crowd, looking for Jim.

"Ugh! Don't tell me we lost him."

CHAPTER 18

Ace of Diamonds

"Shep, you and Cal look for Jim in town here. I'll go to Whiskey Jacks to look for him and talk to Leslie. Hopefully, you will find him."

"Will do. Surely Jim hasn't gone far." Shep, Cal, and Riker walked toward the crowd.

Chris entered Whiskey Jacks and frantically eyed the poker tables for Jim. Seeing Leslie, she approached her. "Leslie, hi. Have you seen Jim? We seemed to have lost him. Did he come back here?"

"No, I haven't seen him." She sighed and glanced around the barroom. "Listen, honey, come on over here. Let's sit down at the bar."

"I don't want a drink. I want to find my father!"

"Ralph, can you get the lady and me two coffees, please."

"Coming up, Les. Whatever you want," the bartender said, cleaning some glassware.

"I know you're upset. But honestly, if Jim is gone, he's gone. If he wants to leave, he knows better than to come back here. Do you know what I'm talkin' about? I think some men just don't want to be found. I've had a little experience in this department, trust me." Leslie lit a cigarette, took a long drag, and blew smoke into the air, taking aim at the ceiling.

"Why would he leave now, just when ..."

"When what?" Leslie put her cigarette in the ashtray, laid her hand on Chris's forearm, and rubbed it.

"Nothing. I just thought Jim wanted to show us around. Plus, I need to get him back to New Jersey to work through some things. Where do you think he went? Does he come here often?"

"Chris, he's been here plenty, playing the tables and all ... but honestly, Jim goes lots of places. He keeps movin', you know? Honestly, he's like a snowbird. Sort of like the rich, I guess. In the winter, he drives his beat-up truck to Vegas for warmth and gambling. In the summer, he returns to his place in the mountains. He always stopped in to say hello to us at Whiskey Jacks."

"His place?" Chris air quoted. "Where is his place?"

"I don't know ... if you can call it that ... he stays somewhere up in these mountains. It's like the forest is Jim's two-million-acre hiding place." Leslie made a big arch with her hands. "When Jim makes a little money at his poker, we might see him. But those lows, when his dough runs out, he retreats to the wilderness. Then, when winter comes, his gambling forces him south again."

Chris closed her eyes slowly, in disappointment overload.

"I can see you're upset. I don't know what to tell you."

"Do you know of any place he would go next or anyone we could see to try to track him?"

Leslie sighed. "Honey, maybe Redfish Lake. He loves to fish there. It seems like he is friendly with the game warden up there, a guy named Elk. I'm sorry. I wish I could help you out more."

"No, Leslie, thank you. Thanks, I appreciate it. If he comes in here, tell him I'm looking for him. Here's my card; it has my mobile number on it. Did you say Elk? Like the animal?"

"Oh, yeah." Leslie waved her hand. "Guess this guy is pretty big, and they nicknamed him that." Leslie looked at Chris's business card. "Fancy title you got there, VP of Administration. And I don't know about cell service up in those mountains."

"Okay, thank you. Thanks for the coffee and the chat." Chris got up from the bar.

"Anytime, honey. Anytime."

Chris met up with Shep and Cal after they had thoroughly combed the town of Ketchum and came up short. "Leslie thought maybe he might be fishing at Redfish Lake. It's a shot in the dark, but it's all we've got."

Within an hour, they were in flight for Stanley, Idaho, the closest town to Redfish Lake and a popular entry into the Sawtooth Mountains.

Stanley's airstrip was in sight. From the air, the half-shaved-grass, half-paved strip could be seen clearly. And parallel to it, the glistening Salmon River. The Sawtooth Mountain range stood majestic, jagged edges topped with snow. As Cal made his approach, the Salmon River's water sparkled as it gently curled out of sight like a winding ribbon.

Once they landed, Cal secured his plane, and Shep located the airport manager, who made small talk. "What brings you to Idaho? Camping, hiking?"

"Well, yes, or rent a cabin, at least. We're looking for someone, a fella named Jim."

"Hmmm. I hope you have some leads on his whereabouts because these mountains cover a big area. Do you know which campsite he might be in?"

"Not a clue," said Shep. He sighed, feeling a bit small in this vast, rugged landscape. Finding Jim was going to be a mountain of a job.

"Well, we'll walk over to town and start there."

"Okay, well, good luck."

"Thanks. Looks like we'll need it," Cal said.

The three of them and Riker walked to town. Loaded down with duffel bags, in the past, they might have passed for settlers or gold diggers coming to the area seeking fortune. They weren't looking for wealth, just for one man.

The town of Stanley, three blocks long and a couple of blocks wide, was a small outpost consisting of the post office, a few restaurants, and a dirt main street called Ace of Diamonds. "Ace of Diamonds. Wouldn't you know?" Chris said.

The three stopped to get a hamburger and some fries. As they ate lunch, Cal said, "I'm going to call home and my office and check to see how everything is going. Hopefully, we can get some good service here in town."

"I'll check in with Hopewell Hill too."

"I'll do the same," Shep said.

They made their respective calls and met at the post office.

"I talked to my wife to check on things at home. Between my son breaking his arm, two patients needing root canals pronto, and us losing Jim, I think I might be more useful back in Jersey. I don't want to disappoint you, but could you two catch commercial flights from Boise back to New Jersey after you finish here?"

"Sure," Chris said. "I understand duty calls. It's not like you have all the time in the world to chase my father around. I just checked in with Hopewell Hill, and everything is okay for now. But it won't be forever, and I will have to return to my day job soon."

"I spoke with Rabbi David, and all seems quiet and steady for now."

"Yes, Cal, by all means. You should get back. Will you be okay flying solo home?" Shep asked.

"Sure, I'll be fine. I'll make my stops and be back in Hopewell in a few days. I'll get a place here for the night and start fresh in the morning. The weather looks clear and sunny, so I should be good for departure in the morning. Thanks for your understanding."

"Oh, man." Shep patted Cal on the shoulder. "We can't thank you enough for flying us out here. Thank you, friend."

Cal smiled at Shep. "No problem. You know I love flying into the backcountry."

They said their goodbyes.

"Well, I can't blame him. He needs to get back," Shep said.

"It's true. Even you may not want to stay on this adventure much longer."

"Riker and me? No, we're here for you, Chris. Besides, I like seeing the more casual side of you. It's pure business at the hospital, but this side is much more intriguing." Shep blushed.

"Thanks for staying with me. You know, Shep, what we need is a car. I grabbed a map at the grocery store. This place is huge, and we may want to travel by car to Redfish Lake. I saw a sign at the post office for Jeep rental. I'll go check it out. We may need some provisions. Here's some cash. Could you pick us up some groceries? I'll meet you back at the post office in an hour."

"Riker and I are on it. Riker, let's get some food. Maybe they'll have some dog treats."

Riker's ears perked up.

After loading up a couple of bags of groceries, Shep and Riker sat on the bench in front of the Stanley Post Office. The sun was beginning to set, and Shep admired the mountains at this point in the day.

Suddenly, the roar of a red-and-orange convertible Jeep Wrangler came around the corner. The paint color on the Jeep was no match for Chris's auburn hair, blowing in the wind. Her hair was like a flame, and she smiled and said, "Going my way, mister?"

"You bet I am."

CHAPTER 19

Redfish Lake Lodge

The sun seeped in through the thin saucers of fog and into Chris's bedroom window. She yawned and rose from her log post bed. Thankfully, she and Shep had found this cabin the night before, one of the last available at Redfish Lake Lodge. As she lay in bed, all seemed quiet until she began to hear humming. *Where is that coming from?* Slipping out of bed with only her camisole on, she tiptoed to the bedroom door. She carefully turned the doorknob to crack the door slightly. The humming was louder as she looked across the hallway to the bathroom. She tried to make out the tune, turning her head to one side.

Shep sang a few bars from "Friends in Low Places."

"Garth Brooks?" She put her forehead on the edge of the door and rolled her eyes. Suddenly, she heard the door opening. Spying while keeping her door mostly closed, she watched Shep emerge. Steam began to waft out from the bathroom. Wearing nothing but a green towel wrapped around his waist, Shep's buff olive-toned upper body was on full chiseled display. As he reached to flip the light off behind him, his V-shaped torso twisted, and his biceps flexed as he hit the switch. Chris slumped back from the crack in the doorway against the wall, biting her lip. It seemed she had just drunk a smooth honey elixir, now radiating from the top of her head down to her red-painted toes. She put her hand to her forehead. *What am I thinking! The hospital chaplain? For gosh sake, Chris, snap out of it.*

Suddenly, with no warning, Riker's half cries could be heard, and his snout came through the door, his body pushing the doorway open to Chris's room with a blast. There she stood, blue cammie and undies, staring straight at Shep in nothing but his green towel. Riker wagged his tail and jumped up on her for a morning greeting. She stumbled back and fell to the bed as he licked her face and wagged his tail.

"Oh, Riker." Shep lunged for Riker, and his towel began to come loose.

"Your towel!" Chris forced her eyes to look away.

Shep quickly grabbed it and promptly readjusted it while getting Riker down. "Oh, Chris, sorry. Riker, back off, boy. He isn't usually this excitable." As Shep stood over her, she was in a tumbled mess with the comforter on the bed, Riker licking and wagging.

"Can you get, get him out? What the heck, Shep. You're half naked!"

"Yeah, well ..." Shep began turning red in the face and fumbled while grabbing Riker's collar in one hand and holding on to his towel in another.

Chris fought with the linens, trying to cover herself. "Can you just get the dog and ..."

"Riker, out. Out the door!" He looked back at Chris with hound-dog eyes. "Sorry. Chris, yeah, this was awkward." He pulled the door shut behind him with a sudden bumbling silence.

Chris fell back on the bed and brought her pillow to her face, screaming into it and pounding her fists. "This couldn't be more embarrassing!"

After she lay there for a few more minutes in unbelief, she got up and pulled some clothes on, brushed her teeth, and put some makeup on. Then she shuffled to the kitchen and began looking for coffee.

Shep, who was already on the deck overlooking the lake, coffee mug in hand, walked inside. "Maybe we can try this again. Good morning, Chris. I sure enjoyed that incredible view this morning."

"Yes, it was something." Chris looked up a little sheepishly. "Oh, wait. What incredible view?"

"I meant you. You should ... come outside. The outside view is just breathtaking. Won't you join me?" Shep was blushing.

Chris nodded toward the lake, ducked under Shep's arm in the doorway, and sipped from her steamy cup.

They stepped out onto the deck, the lake glistening before them.

"Isn't this beautiful? The fresh mountain air does something to you."

"That must explain it. The air."

"Explain what?" Shep asked.

"Oh, nothing. I was thinking that the Hopewell Hill staff would be in a brouhaha if they knew we were in a cabin together in the woods, that's all." Chris grinned.

"Yes, I guess they would. Even if it is a two-bedroom cabin."

The hum of a lake boat could be heard in the distance, and soon water was lapping up against the shore from the wakes.

"What a beautiful place. The water is crystal clear, and those mountains are majestic."

"I was just looking at those mountains and thinking about all the hiking we used to do."

"It sounds like you two had some great times. I can't imagine what losing someone like Annie was like."

"I think you know a thing or two about losing someone."

"Who? Jim? But that was so long ago. I'm a grown woman now."

"Yes, I know, but you were hopeful this time."

"Yes, I was. I guess it's the emotional loss."

"The loss of not having a relationship, you mean?"

"Yeah, that hurts, and it's becoming clearer and clearer, just like that water out there. Jim doesn't want a relationship."

"Maybe Jim doesn't know how. As you know from our work at Hopewell Hill, people in addiction can be consumed by that addiction. They have a hard time seeing out."

"Yes, that's true, but I thought I could break through somehow."

Riker barked at the birds nearby.

"Let's get some breakfast and take a walk. Would you like that? I think Riker is ready to explore."

"Sure, let's do it."

Redfish Lake was big and beautiful. You name it—boating, fishing, kayaking, hiking—they had it. After a delicious breakfast at the lodge, they walked. Shep threw a stick out into the water along the shoreline, and Riker ran to retrieve it. "That a boy, Rike."

Riker shook the water from his body and brought the stick back to Shep for another toss.

"Shep, thank you for all you're doing to help me."

"Sure, Chris. You've been there for me too. I know you're disappointed right now."

"Sometimes I just can't get over how Jim never cared to know about my life."

"I know it's hard, but maybe we have to think about it differently, maybe from his perspective."

"His perspective?"

"I bet Jim has a lot of wounds, don't you think?"

"Yes, I guess if you say it that way, his father leaving the family was a starter."

"Unfortunately, he chose poker to hide from those wounds, or he thought it would bring him the self-worth he never received."

"He wanted to prove he was something, thinking wealth from gambling would bring that. I wish he had sought help." Chris frowned.

"Some things are out of our control. But with Annie's death, I had to let God heal my aching heart one day at a time."

"That's good advice, Shep. I'm glad you've come so far. Right now, I have a father I am aching to hunt down. Where in these bazillion acres are we going to find him?" Chris moved her arms open wide.

"I thought we would go to find that forest ranger Leslie told us about, Elk. We passed the ranger station last night on our way in."

"That's a good plan. Let's head to the Jeep."

They put the Jeep top down and put Riker in the back, and soon, the three of them were driving in the crisp, clear morning to the ranger station. A woman in an olive-drab uniform greeted them.

"Hello, my name is Shep, and this is Chris."

The ranger nodded. "Welcome to the Sawtooth Mountains. How can I help you?"

"Oh, thank you. Sure is different from Jersey out here," Shep said.

"You folks are from Jersey? I have a cousin out there. Are you sightseeing?"

"Well, yes and no. We're looking for someone. Jim Warren is his name. We were told a ranger named Elk might know his whereabouts."

"Oh, Elk. He's out right now, making some rounds. He might be over at Little Redfish Lake. Is there anything I can help you with?"

"No, we'll check there. It's just south of here?"

"Yes, can't miss it, and he probably is checking things out around the campground area."

Chris drove the Jeep and parked in the Mountain View Campground. Little Redfish Lake was stunning, and the October sun displayed the mountains and their lightly snow-capped tips as a postcard-like backdrop.

"Wow, this is gorgeous!"

"It sure is. Come on, Riker."

Chris and Shep walked around the lake and then returned to the campground.

"I think that might be our man over there." Shep nodded toward a ranger truck with the emblem of the Sawtooth Mountains on it and a tank of a man getting out of it.

"Let's head over there."

"Hi there, ranger. My name is Chris. We were told you might be here. Is your name Elk?"

"My real name is Jonathan."

"We're looking for Jim Warren. His friend Leslie said you might know where Jim stays out here."

"Jim? He's the one who nicknamed me Elk. Guess because of my size. I usually lurk around the campground area at night, ensuring things are quiet and not too much ruckus goes on."

"Look, we've come a long way to find Jim. I am his daughter. Do you happen to know where he might be? Is he camping here?"

"Well, I'm not sure. Most of the time, if Jim's truck is here, he's hiked back to do some fishing or ..."

"Or what?" The ranger looked at Chris. "You said you're his daughter?"

"Yes, I am. Chris Warren." Chris shook hands with him.

"Well, guess he uses some kind of settler's cabin on Heart Lake. When he's not in Vegas, he usually parks over there." The ranger pointed toward the parking lot.

Chris put her hand to her brow to shield the sun and looked in that direction. Parked in the lot was a beat-up red camper truck.

"Yep, his truck is there, which means he's in the wilderness or forest. I never worry about Jim. His survival skills, out in nature, are superior to any poker-playing highs he ever had. When surviving in the woods, he's an expert marksman, trapper, hunter, and fisherman. Jim always says there is no need to worry about food when everything a person needs is in nature, just waiting for him. A tent, mess kit, fishing gear, and rifle are all he needs, and the proper hunting and fishing licenses." Elk put his hand on his belt and lifted his heels.

"You said something about Heart Lake. Where is that from here?" Chris asked.

"You take I-75 to Fourth of July Creek Road, then hike the rest of the way in. You might first look around the Salmon River between Little Redfish Lake and I-75. Several fishing spots there along the creeks that pour into the Salmon make for some good fishing."

"Thank you, Elk. You've been a big help."

"No problem. If you find old Jim, tell him he owes me some dough from that last card game."

Chris dropped her head and lowered her eyes. "I'll be sure and tell him."

CHAPTER 20

Bait and Hook

"How do I find myself strapped into a pair of waders in the Salmon River with you, Shep?"

"In my book, it couldn't be better." Shep smiled at Chris as he cast his line along the crystal-clear rapids.

The beautiful Salmon River was home to salmon, steelhead, wild trout, chinook, catfish, and kokanee. The guide at the fishing outfit had been more than happy to set them up with waders and all the fishing gear, and now they stood in the middle of the Salmon River.

"This is spectacular. I can see why Jim would spend time out here." The air was fresh and clean, and the sun hit the rapids, beaming and glistening in every direction. Shep and Chris stood in the river at a bend, evergreens stood across from them at the bank, and beyond them, the Sawtooth Mountains stood as the backdrop.

"This is amazing scenery, but finding Jim along these bazillion miles of river is a long shot. Plus, I think he's probably hiding out where Elk says he goes, up at Heart Lake."

"Maybe, after this, we could hike up there."

"I think that's a good idea." After soaking up the sun and casting their lines a little longer, Chris said, "I think I'll get these chest waders off."

"I think I will too. It might be time for lunch."

They walked to the river's edge together.

Chris sat down on the bank. "Getting this giant human sock off shouldn't be too hard." She pulled the olive-drab straps off and the waders down over her layered clothing beneath. "Sure is a good thing we had these waders on. That water is cold."

"It sure is. I didn't get chilled at all. Did you, Chris?"

"No, I was comfortable." Chris began tugging at her boot. "Now, if I can just get this off."

"Let me help you." Shep came over and gave a tug, putting his hand on the heel and his other hand on the top of her plastic wader boot. "Brace yourself. I'm going to tug on this."

"Okay." Chris put her hands behind her on the grass.

"One, two, three." Shep pulled with a force that took the boot off but landed him with a splash on his rear end in the river.

"Oh, my gosh, Shep. Are you okay?" Chris stood halfway in the chest wader, halfway out, and then stumbled into the water, tripping on her chest wader contraption and onto Shep's body with a splash.

Stunned and dripping wet, Shep smiled. "I'm fine."

Just inches from his face, Chris said, "I don't know what to say."

"Well, I don't know, but ..." Shep leaned up to Chris and looked into her eyes.

Chris looked into his, just inches away from his lips, as she whispered, "This is so, so ..."

"Comfortable," Shep answered.

They lay on the riverbank looking at each other for what seemed like forever before Chris said, "Oh, my gosh." She flung to the side of Shep. "I didn't mean to, uh, oh my." Chris flailed back and forth, splashing everywhere. Half in, half out of her waders.

"Chris, let me help you." Shep reached for her.

"No! No, I've got it." Determined, she began crawling away from Shep, from the riverbank, dousing and splashing herself, pulling her waders along as more cold water flooded inside them. Shep's laughter echoed around the Idaho valley.

Chris turned around with the wader contraption around her, dripping hands on her hips, and said, "What do you think is so funny?"

Shep splashed water back at Chris, and before long, they might as well have been two trout on the side of the Salmon

River flailing to get loose of the fishing line. Both seemed caught between a bait-like attraction and a hook that seemed to be sinking deeper into their hearts.

After they got their waders peeled off their bodies, Chris went to the Jeep for some dry clothes while Shep arranged their picnic lunch. He had had the lodge pack a picnic basket for two with cheese, fruit, sandwiches, and chocolate truffles. Shep spread a blanket on the grass.

As she towel-dried her hair, Chris walked over. "Very thoughtful of you—to arrange this, Shep. Thank you."

"I thought we could use a break from all our man hunting—or Jim hunting."

"Well, we couldn't have picked a more beautiful morning."

Chris sat down under a tree on the blanket. "I can't believe I caught a couple of fish!"

"Too bad we released them. They might have been pretty tasty." Shep hesitated.

"What are you thinking, Shep? Just say it."

"Well, kind of like releasing the fish ... you know you could just let go too, you know?"

"Let go of what? What do you mean?"

"You are amazing, Chris. You have accomplished so much, but it seems you're pushing yourself to stay strong. To be tough. You don't have to do that. Especially with me."

"With you?" Chris turned to look sharply at Shep.

"Honestly, I care about you, Chris, and I don't want to see you get hurt if this all doesn't work out with Jim." He leaned back on the blanket and stared at Chris with brown eyes creamier than the chocolate truffles in front of them. The wind swirled over the rapids and up the embankment, creating a warm breeze that seemed to caress them softly.

"Um, well, I care about you too, Shep. Like friends and all, and I appreciate your concern. I do. But I can handle this. Really." She put a truffle in her mouth and turned away from his gaze, for if she kept looking at him, she was afraid she might just melt in his arms, like the goo of a caramel center.

CHAPTER 21

Heart Lake

Chris parked the Jeep off Fourth of July Creek Road to enter the trailhead to Heart Lake. The afternoon was full of sunshine, yet a chill of autumn was closing in. Shep and Chris wore sweatshirts and jeans to keep warm after their morning dip in the Salmon River.

"The map shows about a two-and-a-half-mile trail up to the lake. Nothing like a good hike. Riker is happy."

"It's beautiful." Chris looked up at the trees and straightened her backpack. "Let's go."

They walked a forest path that wound around a creek. The trail was steep at times. Sometimes they balanced over logs crossing clear babbling water. A dirt path ran next to Heart Creek.

"It's been a long time since I've been in nature like this. I'm so used to being in the office working. This is so refreshing."

"God's creation is refreshing."

"I guess if Jim is out here, I can see why. Except …"

"Except what?"

"Except why would he rather live in isolation out here?"

"We don't know, but at least it's away from gambling."

Chris breathed in the mountain air and pointed at the White Cloud Mountains in the distance. "That's true, and nothing can beat snowcapped mountains like that." The peaks had a dusting of fresh snow on their jagged edges.

They continued hiking. "You know, Chris, you don't have to go this all alone."

"I'm not. You're here with me."

"Yes, I am, gladly."

Chris followed Shep over some stones in a small stream. She took his hand as he helped steady her. "I just wanted a father."

"You have one."

"I know, but …"

"You have a heavenly one who loves you and sees how much you've been hurting. God wants to heal the hurt in your heart. He really does."

"You have hurt too, Shep, over Annie."

"Yes, and God has been with me in my grief. I've taken the time to work through the process with Him."

"I can see that strength in you."

"Come on, Chris. There's a lookout point just beyond here, up to that clearing. I looked at the map, and the top of this trail and Heart Lake are around eight thousand feet above sea level."

The dirt trail narrowed and was thick with Douglas fir, ponderosa pine, and Engelmann spruce trees that smelled like a candle on Christmas morning. Squirrels and birds busied themselves among the branches. Finally, a clearing appeared. Chris and Shep reached it and stood together.

Chris gave an audible gasp as she looked at the vantage point beyond. "Oh, I've never seen anything so beautiful. It really is a heart." The alpine lake shimmered in the afternoon light before them, like an emerald gem shining with every hue of blue and aqua possible. The edge of the lake outlined a perfect heart shape. Chris looked at the water and wanted to dive into its beauty, into the heart of it. "It takes my breath away. It's like a fantasy novel, but there it is. A huge heart."

"Makes you want to dive in, doesn't it?" Shep put his hand on Chris's shoulder.

"Yes, it does. Do you see any cabin along the water?"

Both Shep and Chris looked along the edges.

"Oh wait, where is that smoke coming from? It looks as though it's coming from that little shanty there. See it? To the right, Chris?"

"Where?"

A small plume of smoke rose and wisped in the air. The wood of the little shanty by the side of the lake took on blueish and purple tones. "Yes. I do see it. It's nothing more than a lean-to. That thing would have no running water; that's for sure.

Surely, that's not what Elk described. How would anyone live in that?" The old shack looked like it had been built by fur trappers or gold diggers.

"Well, I don't know, but someone has a fire going."

Just then, an eagle soared above the lake. His whistle and cawing sounds cut through the stillness in the air like a knife. "Caw, caw." The eagle's wingspan was so large as it soared above, making a screeching sound. The wilderness responded in silence. It was like some kind of warning. Beware. For Chris, it was hair raising. If Jim was in that shanty, in his makeshift home in the woods, there was nothing else to do but face this. Face Jim. But still, she couldn't believe her father lived in such a place in the wilderness. She thought of her daily life and how absolutely and utterly different her life was from this. She spent every day at the hospital trying to save people while Jim sat in complete solitude in this shack at the forest's edge. How could this be? Peaceful and all, yes. But in check with reality? No. Her heart burned with anger at the truth of it. If this was where he had been hiding out, if Jim was in that shanty, she wanted to talk to him.

"Let's go. Let's get this over with."

"Let me take your hand. This path is steep."

"I've got this." Chris then turned and looked at Shep. When she looked at his kind face and gentle smile, she gave him her hand and trusted him, for this moment, for this journey.

CHAPTER 22

The Color of My Heart

The sunshine reflected perfect hues of blue and shades of green from Heart Lake's edge. The mirror reflection of the trees on the water was postcard material. As they neared the shanty, the smokey scent from the fire became more robust, and a light breeze swept their faces.

"This place looks pretty run down."

Chris felt uneasy as she walked toward it. "What will I say to Jim if he's in there?"

"Just tell him you're here for him."

"Or maybe I should ask him why he left us in that sheep town, wondering where he was. Or why we've had to hike all these miles to track him down. Maybe that's what I should ask him."

"Just go to the door and call his name."

Chris took one look at the shanty in front of her. She turned to look at the lake on her left, the wind making mini ripples on the water. The stillness of the forest. They stood alone, she and Shep.

Shep nodded. "You can do this, Chris."

Chris turned slowly and looked at Shep, his soft eyes reassuring her. She pressed her lips together and put her fist to the splintered wood. She banged on it. "Jim, it's me. Chris." She banged on it again. "Jim! Are you in there?"

Silence.

"Jim, Shep and I are here. Elk told us you might be here."

Nothing.

Chris ducked down a bit and peeked through cracks in the slanted doorway. She grabbed one of the wooden slats and pulled the door open. Shep followed.

A lantern illuminated the inside. A fire was slowing to hot coals. A coffeepot, a camp mess kit, and an iron skillet were next to the fire. A wooden chair and table stood next to it; both looked handmade from nearby forest trees. A cot was near with a gray woolen blanket snugly covering it. Jim's duffel bag lay near it on the floor.

Chris went over and touched the tin coffeepot. "The coffee is warm, the fire is started, his duffel bag is here, there is his Skoal container, but no Jim."

"And here is his fishing gear." Next to the cot were a knife, sling, waders, fishing basket, fly fishing pole, and fishnet.

As Chris turned to look near the bed, she gasped and covered her mouth in shock. Above his cot were all kinds of pictures. Of Chris. "What in the world? How did he get all this!" Pinned to the wood were newspaper articles of Chris in grade school and high school, cheerleading pictures, a Polaroid snapshot of the day she moved into her dorm at college, pictures of when she was little, and a picture of her in her first car, that blue Capri. Photos of her with her prom date and high school and college graduation pictures. Every significant moment in Chris's life was displayed on the wooden slats above Jim's bed. "Here are the pictures I just gave him, out on the bed. This is crazy."

Shep leaned in to look at all the pictures of Chris more closely. "What's crazy is how you wore your hair back then, and ..."

Chris moved closer to look at the same picture from high school. "And what?"

"And ..." Shep turned to Chris and whispered, "How beautiful you are. That's what's crazy."

Chris could already feel her heart pumping when they neared this shanty, but now she thought it was about to beat out of her chest.

He took her into his arms, and she let him. The moment seemed beyond their control. Then Shep held her and gently and lovingly kissed her.

Chris melted in his embrace, and their lips caressed each other in a sweet release.

Then she whispered to him, "This is going to be a problem."

"Maybe or maybe not." Shep raised his eyebrow at her.

"Ugh, well." She fidgeted and stammered back, straightening her sweatshirt. "We can't do this. Now. We need to figure all this out, Shep." She turned back to the table.

"You're right, Chris. Let's focus." They gained composure and began looking around the cabin again.

"Look, a card from a casino in Vegas, his old tin poker box, Skoal, and Grandmother Rose's Bible." Chris rubbed her fingers over the faded tin poker box. "I remember this box from when I was a kid." She opened it, and her eyes widened. The blue poker chips with ridges, a deck of cards and wallet-sized pictures of Chris from every grade, and a key marked for Stanley Post Office box number 56. "This is unbelievable. Why did he not say anything? Or better yet, how did he get all this stuff about me?"

"I don't know, but it sure looks like he always had you on his mind, Chris."

"Mom was the only one who could have mailed him these things."

"Maybe so. That says a lot about Helen."

"It really does." Chris stared in shock.

"Maybe Jim is outside." Riker could sense their urgency and whined a little. Shep said, "Come on, Riker. Let's go."

Shep, Chris, and Riker began searching outside at the lake's edge.

"Jim! Jim!" Chris called.

Riker began sniffing more near the wooded trails.

"I don't see him anywhere on the lake."

"I don't either."

Suddenly, they could hear Riker barking.

"That's Riker!" Shep darted toward his barking, and Chris followed.

"Over here. Over here." Shep waved Chris to Riker. Through trees and forest floor, away from the lake, and deeper into the woods. Riker was barking and circling.

"Jim! Jim."

He was lying between trees. Blood covered his shirt and chest.

"What happened?"

"Chris," Jim whispered.

Chris dropped to her knees and put her hand on Jim's shoulder.

Shaking, she said, "Jim, what happened?"

Shep came to Jim's side.

"Shep? How did you find me?" Jim muttered.

"Big Elk told us where you might be. We followed the trail here. What happened to you? You're bleeding."

"An ole mule deer had his antler rack caught between these trees over here." Jim's breathing was labored. "I could hear him back at camp, struggling to get free. I should have shot him. Put him out of his misery." Jim's rifle lay on the ground.

Chris looked at the puncture wound on Jim's chest, right over his heart. "Did you try to get him free?"

"Yes. Freed him, but he lunged for me."

"We've got to get him some help. Shep, try your phone. Can you get a signal?"

Jim's moaning increased.

"I'm right here, Jim." Chris touched Jim's brow.

"Nothing. Dead. No service… Riker and I will head back to the Jeep and to Stanley for help."

"The keys are in my backpack. I'll stay here with Jim. Hurry."

"We'll go as fast as we can. Jim, you hang on, you hear?"

"Sure, Shep. Sure." Jim was sweating, and his breathing was difficult.

Chris watched Shep and Riker run from the scene as Jim's breathing became shallower. The leaves rustled in the light breeze, all the golden colors of yellow working with the light to form rays of sunshine upon them.

"I've had some time. Time to think, Chris. About us. Me and that old mule deer. We're the same. I sure made a wreck of things. Always trying to do things my own way."

"Jim, I have so many questions about this place, this lake. But there is no time. You have to save your strength."

"I always came here to get away. No poker out here. No place to lose, I guess."

"Dad, I saw all the pictures of me in your cabin. Where did you get those?"

"Helen. Good Helen. You done good, Spud. I'm proud of you. Even though I wasn't around for you, you were with me in that cabin through those pictures."

"I just wish you could have been with me all those times growing up."

"I stayed away. You didn't need me messing things up. I chose a gambler's life. After a while, I just didn't want you to really see me. See the man I had become. " Jim shrieked in pain and began shivering.

"I'll get your blanket. I'll be right back." Chris ran back to the shanty, got the blanket from Jim's cot, and was back at his side in minutes. As she covered Jim, she noticed beyond them a dot of red in the distance. Indian paintbrush.

"You rest. Shep will bring help soon."

"You two make a good team. Stick together; don't let a good thing go like I did. You and Helen were the best things to ever happen to me. Hold on to that, Shep. Listen, Spud, I may not make it out of this." Jim went unconscious.

"Jim! Jim!" Chris shouted, and tears began.

Jim's eyes opened a little. "I'm here. I'm here."

"Dad, I want you to know something." Tears streaked her face. "I ... I forgive you."

A tear dropped from Jim's eye as he nodded. He smiled, and then the color faded from his face. And he was gone.

Tears like raindrops flowed as Chris reached down to kiss her dad on the cheek. Through her sobs, she felt a wave of peace settle on her. As she looked up, the Indian paintbrush flower moved gently in the wind, like an old friend comforting her. "Father God, I know you are here with me. With us. Thank you." She took the blanket and slowly covered Jim through her tears.

CHAPTER 23

Calling Home

"Mom, I've got some news."

"Are you calling from Idaho, Chris? I've been wondering how it's been going out there."

"Yes, Mom. I need to tell you something."

"What? Oh, no, Chris. I don't like the sound of your voice. What happened?"

"Dad has died."

"Oh, Chris. What? What happened?"

"Mom, it's a long story, and I'll fill you in on everything when I return. We lost track of Jim a little bit while we were out here. But we tracked him down to his place."

"His place?"

"The place in the woods. You know, Mom. You must know about it."

"No, Chris. I don't know about any place in the woods of your father's."

"You must."

"Chris, why are you saying that? I must?"

"Because all my pictures of me growing up were plastered everywhere inside that cabin!"

"What?"

"Mom, how did he get those, and why didn't you tell me you were sending them?"

"Chris, oh honey, I never imagined."

"Never imagined what?"

"Look, Chris, all I had was a PO box from a letter your dad wrote me about a year or two after we left. It was the same one Mamma Rose had years ago. I wasn't sure it was still a box he kept, but I knew it was out at Stanley. I guess I hoped he would receive the things I sent. I kept sending to it over the years, hoping Jim hadn't moved on. I just wanted him to see you growing up."

"Well, you probably should have told me or asked my permission."

"Honey, forgive me. Do you know how brokenhearted you were when your dad never reached out? Well, I was doubly brokenhearted to watch that happen. I thought sending those pictures would help him know how wonderful you were growing up and are. I had hoped he would reach out. After each one I mailed to him, I said a prayer. A prayer that this one would make a difference. This note, this picture of you would make him stop gambling, change his ways, and be involved with you."

Chris could hear her mom softly crying on the other end of the phone. "Mom, it's okay. I'm sorry if I lashed out at you. The whole thing has been so overwhelming. But it's over. It's over."

"How did he die?"

"Truthfully, I think of a lonely, broken heart. A lonely, broken heart."

"Chris, I am so sorry. Are you okay? Do you need me to come out?"

"Mom, I'm okay. Really. I will just see about his final arrangements and then be home. Shep is with me. If it's any consolation, I forgave Jim ... Dad. He heard those words from me and accepted them."

"Oh, that's wonderful. Honey, I hope you can forgive me too. I was only trying to bridge the gap between you and your dad."

"I know, Mom, I know. And I guess I'm glad he saw me through those pictures. He sure had them up everywhere in his little hut in the woods. It's on a lake, a heart-shaped lake. The place is quite beautiful. Very peaceful."

"That's good."

"I'm glad I came out here. I guess in some strange way, I was with him all along through those pictures you sent."

"Hopefully that helped more than we will ever know."

"Maybe, Mom."

"And Shep? Was he a help?"

Chris stroked her hair and smiled. "Yes, he was a help, for sure. He's quite something."

"Quite something, yes. The one time I met Shep at the hospital, I would say he's a handsome something."

"Mom! Honestly!"

"Well, I'm just saying the truth. I am glad you were not alone out there. What about the pilot?"

"Cal. He had to fly back a little early due to pressing things at home."

"Oh, that left you and Shep alone to try to find Jim?"

"Yes, for a few days."

"Hmm. Well, that was convenient."

"Mom, here you go again at a time like this."

"Oh, Chris, you know a mother knows."

"Knows what?"

"It's just a hunch I have, that's all."

CHAPTER 24

Canyon of My Heart

A few weeks later

Chris could see lots of activity around Grace Chapel as she entered. Shep was near the altar, moving things around, and a florist was bringing white ribbons and greens to the altar. She walked outside for more supplies from her van.

"Hi, Shep. What's going on around here?"

"Oh, hi, Chris. It's a big day here, you know. We have a wedding this afternoon. You look very nice in that dress."

Chris smiled at Shep as she fiddled with the pearls against her black dress. "Thank you."

"A wedding. Who's getting married?"

"Olivia and Allen. You know Olivia was a patient a few months back. She was discharged while we were in Idaho. Seems we did our job, and she's much better. She and her fiancé, Allen, want to move forward with each other together."

Chris smiled. "Well, it doesn't get any better than that, does it?"

"It's great. It should be a very nice wedding. What do you have there in your hand? I hope it's not another report you want from me?"

"Report? No, just something I thought I would add to the *H O P E* book." Chris stammered a little.

"Be my guest." Shep moved his hand toward the altar in an ushering way.

"Before I do that, Shep, I just want to thank you. Thank you for staying in Idaho with me while I took care of my dad's final arrangements. He would have been pleased with me spreading his ashes over the Salmon River. That's what he would have wanted. I'm so glad you were with me."

"I think he would have been real happy with that too. We performed a beautiful little service on the riverbank, just the two of us. I know, Chris, this may not have worked out as you had wanted. You really wanted him to fully rehabilitate. I know that."

"Yes, that would have been nice. To get to know Jim. Really know him. Those last few minutes with him somehow covered years of doubt and regret. God was with us. There was peace. I couldn't have done it without you." Chris looked around to make sure the florist was outside. Leaning over, she kissed Shep on the cheek.

"Well, you're welcome. It was some journey, and I can't think of anyone I would rather have accompanied than you. We were in a different world in Idaho, but now we're back at work."

"Yes, back to work." Chris sighed a bit.

"You know, Chris, since returning, I've been doing some thinking. I've been thinking about pizza. Pizza from Antonio's."

"That's what you've been thinking about? Pizza?"

"Yes. That's not the only thing, but I could tell you more about it when I come over. Could I bring over a pizza tonight after I'm done here?"

Chris looked around. "Why, I guess a little discussion over pizza would be okay."

"Later tonight?"

"Don't you have this wedding?"

"I do, but after they start dancing at the reception, it's perfectly okay if I slip out."

"Okay, I guess tonight works."

"I'll need your address."

"Sure. I'm on Twelve Madison, an older home I remodeled."

"I know the street. How about eight o'clock?"

"Eight it is."

She began walking down the aisle toward the altar, then turned back and looked at him, smiled, and walked to the front of the chapel.

Shep watched Chris stand and slowly open the *H O P E* book with reverence. She softly brushed the edges of the pages former patients had left, stories of healing and hope. She added her pages and then closed the book.

"See you later," she whispered, waved, and slipped out the side entrance.

"See you tonight." Shep waved.

Alone, just he and Riker, Shep walked to the front and ran his fingers across the book. "Rike, I can't help myself." He opened it to the page Chris had just added.

Canyon of My Heart

The piercing knife of earthly fatherlessness and abandonment had cut a canyon in my soul. Into my very heart.

In my inner self. Deep and jagged and raw was this. At first, oozing with hurt and fleshlike bleeding. Puffy and bruised, it was from the initial abandonment. Hope was lost. No balm seemed sufficient.

Then. You came. With my surrender and forgiveness offered, You breathed your warm, healing wind into the deep crevasse of my heart. You made purple hemorrhages smooth and hardened my swollen, jagged edges. You made minerals spring forth from the wound with vibrant colors where there was once bleeding. Your Holy Spirit calmed the wound with hope, like no other.

Now the canyon exists, but you made beauty out of it. I fly with honor and soar with dignity along its glorious ledges. With my wings, I spread wide to embrace your loving mercy. I feel your wind on the face of my heart. Now, glory revealed. As I fly, I breathe in your healing fragrances and show you my rich, splendorous sidewalls.

And as I soar through this calm and peaceful canyon valley that you made beautiful, I sing. And singing, I say Thank You—ABBA FATHER!

—*Chris Warren*

Shep closed the *H O P E* book. He sighed a peaceful sigh and looked up at the stained-glass window. "You sure are making beauty out of this whole situation, unexpected beauty, Lord. I only hope she feels the same way about me."

CHAPTER 25

Pizza and Ice Cream

Chris opened her front door to Shep standing, hands full, in a leather jacket and jeans.

"Pizza delivery." Shep smiled, holding a bouquet of yellow and pink roses. He had a pizza box in the other hand and, on top of that, ice cream from the Hopewell Creamery, mint chocolate chip.

"This is a full-scale delivery. What a surprise, with flowers and ice cream included! I see you even have a delivery truck, too." She nodded toward Shep's Ford truck, parked in her driveway. "Come in, and you too, Riker. How was the wedding?"

"Very nice, just two kids in love. I'm a little hungry. I can't say I had much to eat there. I'm glad you were up for pizza tonight." Shep looked around as he walked in. "And what a comfy home you have." He looked around.

"Oh, thanks. It's home." The two white linen couches faced each other with dusty blue and cream pillows around. Wooden beams met in the center of the ceiling, matching the wooden hearth over the fireplace.

"I thought you might be in an upscale apartment or something. Do you realize we only live a few miles apart?"

"Come in. We can put the pizza over here." Chris set the pizza box on her farm table, already set with wine glasses and soft blue placemats with napkins to match. "I started a fire in the fireplace. It's starting to get chilly."

"Yes, it is. This is very cozy. Riker, you better behave yourself. We don't want to get kicked out before we even have pizza, boy."

Riker tilted his head, went over, and laid down next to the fire as if he could catch Shep's vibe to be out of sight.

"Let's sit."

They sat down, and Chris poured the Cantina red wine.

"Can I offer grace?"

"Absolutely."

"Lord, thank you for our safe return. Thank you for this time together tonight. Even though parts of our Idaho adventure were so hard, most of it was beautiful. We thank you for the healing you brought and what you did for Chris and Jim. Amen."

"You know, I love that."

"Love what?" Steam rolled out as Shep opened the pizza box, revealing the pepperoni pizza with green peppers.

"That smells amazing. Nothing like pizza from Antonio's. I love that you always say grace before your meals. I think I'll adopt that."

"You will, will you?" Shep took a slice of the pie, held it folded together, and took his first bite.

Chris had a salad ready, and she scooped some with the wooden spoons onto their plates.

"Are you back into the groove at the office?" Shep asked after swallowing his first bite.

"Getting there. How about the chapel office and patients? Did you finally relieve Rabbi David?"

"Oh yes, finally. David was happy to help, but I think he was ready for the break from the daily patient load of the Hill. I told him only till next time; he wasn't off the hook."

"Till next time you go hunting a father down? Does that seem likely?"

"It may not be a father, but who knows? Right now, I have an interesting problem right on campus."

"Oh really? Right on campus?"

"Yep." Shep nodded.

"What does the problem seem to be?"

"It's not actually a problem, but a person that may pose a problem."

"A person?"

"A woman."

"Oh really? A woman? Now this sounds interesting. Tell me about her, Shep."

"Well, she can seem quite intimidating to some. She is strong. Smart and beautiful. Gorgeous, actually, but ..."

"But what?" Chris held a crooked smile.

"Beneath that tough exterior, I think she really can be quite the softy."

"Softy? Really?"

Shep nodded.

"What would you do about having a relationship with this woman on campus? You must know about the rules on these things."

"Absolutely. No dating of hospital personnel. No problem for me, though, since I don't work directly for the hospital." Shep gave a big grin.

"How convenient. But of course, don't you think there would be a lot of unnecessary talk between all the staff if you should proceed with a relationship with this woman?"

"I will just have to rough it out, and of course, she will too. I feel for her more, being she is so high up and all." He gave a wink.

"Plus, dating the chaplain could be considered scandalous, perhaps?"

"Perhaps, except the chaplain happens to be single. But there is one other thing. This woman has been dating someone else before, I am told. I'm not sure what to do about that. What would you advise?"

"I advise that you be direct. Tell this woman you're interested in that you care for her, and see her response. If it's positive, then I don't think you need to worry about Spencer. The other man, that is." Chris cleared her throat and began to blush.

Shep stood from the table. "Let's take our ice cream over by the fire."

He took the container with two spoons stuck in the carton and offered his hand to Chris. They sat on the rug by the fire, leaning on two big throw pillows.

They dipped out scoops with their spoons and silently looked into the fire, swallowing the delicious frozen delight.

"It really might be complicated, though, Shep. You might ought to consider your other options. This woman sounds a little high maintenance, maybe?"

"Maybe. I've thought of that. But I still have a problem."

"What is that?"

"The problem is, despite everything, I'm falling madly in love with her." Shep's browns stared into Chris's greens.

"Despite everything."

"Yes."

"Well," Chris whispered, "I guess there is just one thing to do."

"Yes, only one thing to do."

Shep dipped his finger into the green ice cream and put some on her nose.

"Really? That's your one thing?" Chris dipped her finger into the ice cream and put some on Shep's nose.

They began laughing as Shep put the next dip into her mouth, and she matched that to his lips, and before long, they were kissing and eating ice cream all at once. The fire was raging, Riker was barking, and their hearts were melting.

The End

A NOTE FROM THE AUTHOR

ear reader, do you find that, strangely, fiction is an excellent tool for dealing with reality? It helps us take a step back, imagine how we might like life to be, or learn from someone else's mistakes so we can examine our own. Because honestly, our own circumstances might just be a bit painful. Fiction allows us to laugh at the absurd and cry for our characters in their sorrow. Hopefully, when we read the last line, we can close the book and be better and feel better that someone else knew our very own pain, understood, and, by golly, found a solution. Eureka!

As I write this, it will soon be daybreak. I rose in the dark and searched for the moon out my back window, as I sometimes do when feeling lonely or afraid in the middle of the night. No moon was there, but I could see the light from the sky anyway, so I moved to the house's front window, and there it was. Not a full moon, no, but a thin crescent one hanging there lighting the way, my way, with a bright star next to it.

Maybe you are reading this and feel you have lost your way in the night, in the night of addiction to something, or your loved one is completely sinking before your eyes. Hold fast, sweet one. The moon is still hanging in the sky, and the stars are shining somewhere. Just look up. Take hold of the greatest love in all the world. God loves us. He wants to shine on you and be your beacon in the wilderness. Reach out your hand and take hold of His.

—Stacy

ACKNOWLEDGMENTS

Many have asked about my writing journey. Beginning with my first fiction writing course at Gotham Writers in NYC and becoming a founding board member of the Northeast Chapter of American Christian Fiction Writers group, writing friends and groups have supported me immensely. Several critique writing groups followed. Special times like hanging out at a writer's retreat in the Poconos with writing friends Carrie Turansky, Cher Gatto, and Terri McAdoo have been a joy.

Thank you to the ReNEW conference team, Dr. Saundra Dalton-Smith's Invitation to Identity, and Carol Kent's Speak Up conference and certification class. Thank you to Deborah Keiser at Reedsy.com for a developmental edit that pushed me to the finish line—just what I needed.

To my publisher, Redemption Press, and Athena Dean Holtz and Ross Holtz for first reading my story and sending me the encouraging "Yes, this is the fiction we like to publish." Thank you to Carol Mertz Tetzlaff at Redemption Press University for teaching me and other writers how to market our books. Thank you to Tiffani for your talented and creative cover design. I thank Jennifer Fedler, my project manager; Inger Logelin and Ray Dittmeier for editing; and the whole Redemption Press team.

Thank you to Robyne Gardner Locke and Eleanor Braun, who prayed in advance of publication about so many of this book's details. Those prayers moved mountains.

To George,

Thank you for loving me. When you took me on our first date to a nuclear reactor, I, after taking a minute to look, replied, "Aren't you going to take me to dinner?" It's been an absolute adventure since! I am so happy we have been on this journey called life together.

To Sarah and Trey,

The word love took on a whole new dimension when you were born. Thank you for your love, your laughter, and for just being the beautiful human beings you are!

To Mom,

When I think of you, I think of sunshine. To be around you is a joy and blessing to us all. Thank you for saying yes to a path of a better life. It took courage, lots of it.

To John and Sherie,

In good times and bad times, we stick together. Love you and so thankful for you.

To Mama Ruby, Aunt Floy, Grace, and Ethan, pillars of faith,

You showed me such love in planting a garden and attempted to teach me to sew. You loved us through your Sunday table of bountiful food graced with beauty.

DISCUSSION QUESTIONS

1. In the opening chapter, is there a glimpse of what will come? Is there also hope for what life could be like if Jim makes different choices?

2. A twenty-five-year absence—how has Chris positively funneled this time? When Chris confronts her father, what do you think her initial feelings are? Have you had the experience of reuniting with a family member? What was that like?

3. What type of restoration do you think Shep could be alluding to when he tells Jim about his truck restoration? What keeps Jim, and sometimes us, from buying into the idea that God can fight our battles?

4. Why do you think Jim cannot see how much Chris wants a healthy relationship with him?

5. How is Shep trying to reach out to Jim by taking him to the airport hangar? Does Jim gain a physical lesson from Shep and a deeper understanding of him?

6. How does the story of Shep adopting Riker resonate with Jim? What are some glimpses into Jim's past, and how could this be affecting his current behavior? Do you think if we knew what others went through in their childhood, it might change how we see them now?

7. How is Shep showing Chris a way to deal with her pain? How are Shep's offbeat ways sometimes amusing but often annoying to Chris? Does she find some appeal to it?

8. Shep is hunting for Jim, and he uses all his resources to find him. What kind of love is Shep displaying for Jim? Is Jim so deep into his addiction he can't see what others are doing for him? Have you known someone like Jim?

9. How is the story Jim tells of Old Gray similar to Jim's life story? What does God do on our behalf?

10. How have Jim's actions affected his relationship with Chris? What does Chris find inside the cabin her father has been hiding in? If forgiveness is offered and received in a problematic relationship, how does that change the one who forgives?

11. In the poem Chris leaves in the book of hope, what has Chris discovered? How has this changed her perspective on herself and on her father, Jim? Have you found that God can heal and bless you even through a troublesome relationship?

Follow Stacy Ladyman on **f**

Sign up for her newsletter at stacyladyman.com

If you or someone you know has a gambling problem,
call 1-800-GAMBLER
For support for families affected by
a gambling addiction:
GAM-ANON, gam-anon.org

Order Information

Additional copies of this book can be ordered
wherever Christian books are sold
or at stacyladyman.com